What Are You Afraid Of?

Stories About Phobias

What Are You Afraid Of?

Stories About Phobias

edited by Donald R. Gallo

THE WORLD
ON THE OTHER
SIDE O' THE
MIRROR
...

CANDLEWICK PRESS
CAMBRIDGE, MASSACHUSETTS

Introduction copyright © 2006 by Donald R. Gallo
Compilation copyright © 2006 by Donald R. Gallo
"The Door" copyright © 2006 by Alex Flinn
"Calle de Muerte" copyright © 2006 by Ron Koertge
"Thin" copyright © 2006 by Joan Bauer
"D'arcy" copyright © 2006 by Angela Johnson
"Claws and Effect" copyright © 2006 by David Lubar
"Rutabaga" copyright © 2006 by Nancy Springer
"Bang, Bang, You're Dead" copyright © 2006 by Jane Yolen and
Heidi E. Y. Stemple
"No Clown Zone" copyright © 2006 by Gail Giles
"Instructions for Tight Places" copyright © 2006 by Kelly Easton
"Fear-for-All" copyright © 2006 by Neal Shusterman

First edition 2006

Library of Congress Cataloging-in-Publication Data
What are you afraid of? / edited by Donald R. Gallo. — 1st ed.
p. cm.
Summary: Presents ten short stories by well-known authors featuring teenagers with phobias, including fear of gaining weight, fear of clowns, and fear of cats.
Contents: The door / by Alex Flinn — Calle de Muerte / by Ron Koertge — Thin / by Joan Bauer — D'arcy / by Angela Johnson — Claws and effect / by David Lubar — Rutabaga / by Nancy Springer — Bang, bang, you're dead / by Jane Yolen and Heidi E. Y. Stemple — No clown zone / by Gail Giles — Instructions for tight places / by Kelly Easton — Fear-for-all / by Neal Shusterman.
ISBN 0-7636-2654-6
1. Fear — Juvenile fiction. 2. Phobias — Juvenile fiction. 3. Teenagers — Juvenile fiction. 4. Short stories. [1. Fear — Fiction. 2. Phobias — Fiction. 3. Teenagers — Fiction. 4. Short stories.] I. Gallo, Donald R.
PZ5.W4965 2006
[Fic] — dc22   2004062874

2   4   6   8   10   9   7   5   3   1

Printed in the United States of America

This book was typeset in Garamond.

Candlewick Press
2067 Massachusetts Avenue
Cambridge, Massachusetts 02140

visit us at www.candlewick.com

For M. Jerry Weiss,
fearless promoter of
books for teens

ACKNOWLEDGMENTS

This book exists because another one doesn't. Author Alex Flinn asked me if I'd be interested in reading a short story that she had written for an anthology whose publication had been canceled. Being a fan of Alex Flinn's novels, I certainly was interested. And I liked the story—a lot.

Her story deals with a high school student who, for good reason, becomes afraid to go to school, but the feeling gets worse, so that eventually he becomes afraid to even venture outside his family's house. He has what's called agoraphobia.

I was at that time in the middle of working on an anthology about teenage immigrants (which became *First Crossing*), and Flinn's story, unfortunately, did not fit that focus. But the story stuck in my mind, popped up from time to time, wouldn't let me forget it. Then one day my wife, C.J., said, "Why don't you do a book about phobias?" *Click.* Perfect idea: a book of stories about teenagers suffering from and dealing with various fears. So thank you, Alex Flinn, for getting this book started. And thank you, C.J., for providing the direction.

I am also grateful to all the writers who contributed their stories that make this book possible. Their enthusiasm, writing talent, and willingness to revise helped make this a pleasurable project.

Thanks are also due to Deb Wayshak, Liz Bicknell, and the production staff at Candlewick for their support and guidance in getting this book into print.

What are you afraid of? Everyone is afraid of something—maybe it's spiders or walking through a certain section of the city. But that doesn't mean you have a phobia. There is probably a good reason you fear spiders: a childhood friend of yours was bitten by a brown recluse spider and you saw how badly the bite swelled and hurt your friend. As for that one section of the city, you stay out of it, especially at night, because of its high rate of muggings, reported drug use, store robberies, and carjackings. Phobias, on the other hand, are fears blown completely out of proportion—causing extreme reactions.

For example, being in an elevator that is stuck between floors will certainly be a concern for most people, especially until they know that someone has realized the problem and has contacted the right people to fix the elevator and/or rescue them quickly. But for those who have claustrophobia—who fear enclosed spaces—the stalled elevator quickly begins to feel like a small box without air . . . and the walls are closing in. Their heartbeat increases rapidly; their skin begins to sweat; their vision narrows; their throat gets dry; they feel their insides shrinking; they lose all sense of proportion. Those people are not just concerned, like the other passengers. Those people are terrified.

To explore situations like that, I invited several well-known authors to write stories with teenagers as the main characters. Each writer got to choose his or her phobia. The results were surprising as well as satisfying. While a few authors looked inside themselves at their own fears, others looked outside for situations that would result in an interesting story. They looked at how fear affects their teenage characters, what may have caused that fear, how the characters try to deal with their fear, and in some cases, how that fear is eventually overcome.

I was surprised to see that no one in these stories is terrified of spiders (arachnophobia) or snakes and other reptiles (herpetophobia). And no one has some of the other common fears: fear of strangers (xenophobia), fear of thunder (ceraunophobia), or fear of flying (aviophobia). But as you will soon see, in addition to Alex Flinn's tense story about a boy with agoraphobia, there are stories about nine other phobias: Joan Bauer tells us about a young woman's fear of gaining weight. Kelly Easton's character is claustrophobic. Gail Giles takes a humorous approach to a teen's lifetime fear of clowns. Angela Johnson looks at the experiences of a boy who is afraid of string. Ron Koertge's character is not just afraid to cross the street; he is unable to even put one foot off the curb. David Lubar takes a humorous look at a boy's fear of cats, but his character isn't laughing. Nancy Springer's character has an aversion to sharp knives. Jane Yolen and her daughter, Heidi E. Y. Stemple, explore a high-school student's fear of speaking in public. And Neal Shusterman's story includes a variety of phobias suffered by students in a special school until one unique student comes along.

What makes these teenage characters so afraid, and how do they deal with their fears? You'll have to read to find out. But you need not read the stories in the order they are presented. Don't be afraid to jump around. Choose whichever fear grabs your interest and read on. Don't be afraid to try something new. Along the way, you might want to explore your own fears. What are you afraid of?

Don Gallo

Cameron knows he can't stay inside forever.
But one thing stands in his way. . . .

The Door

. . . . .

Alex Flinn

The door has been closed for a week now.

At first, after Mom and David left, I still went out on the doorstep. Maybe even the walkway. And once—oh, once—I walked clear to the street, across the grass—green, clover-dotted, tickling the tops of my toes while the panic invaded and played with my lungs and my heart and my mind until I felt I would faint, but I knew I wouldn't, couldn't, and then I ran inside and slammed the door and felt . . . better.

Crazy, but better.

But even so, the next day, I got as far as the path. The end of the path, really. I stood, feeling the small, shiny rocks under my feet. I *looked* at the street, at least. And when the panic immersed me, I didn't waste time. I went inside and slammed the door and felt . . . worse.

But now the door has been closed for a week.

I stare out the window at the grass—long, unmowed. Unmowed because *I* was supposed to be doing the mowing.

"At least he'll be around to mow the grass." That's what Mom said the day they left, standing in the front hall, suitcases packed. "Oh, Cameron, I wish you were coming with us. Or that you'd gone to camp with Sean. I hate leaving you alone like this."

"Camp is for babies," I said, trying to breathe, trying to calm the fear that leaped in my heart at the thought of going to camp. I didn't want them to leave. But I knew Mom had to. I'd heard them fighting about it all week.

"He's a big boy, Miriam," my stepfather, David, said, hefting his suitcase onto his shoulder and checking his watch. "You coddle him with this homeschooling. He's getting lazy, barely leaving the house anymore. He's seventeen, and it's only a month. He can walk anywhere in town. Do him good."

"I suppose . . ." Mom's hand traced a path through my hair. "I wish you were coming. David's mother would love to see—"

"I can't go," I said too quickly. David had opened the door, and I backed away from the rush of air, hot air. "I don't want to go to David's mother's. I don't want to go to camp. I don't want to go anywhere."

But as the suffocating humidity blasted my face, I thought, *I can't go.* Did they really not see it? It seemed so stupid, but I was glad they were stupid because it would be too embarrassing for them to know the truth, that I couldn't leave the house.

Mom said, "You can look through those college catalogs."

"Yeah."

David swung a garment bag at me. "Here. Take this."

And with both of them standing there, and me trying to act normal, I'd made it out to the car and back, though I'd taken three bags at once so I wouldn't require a second trip. But at least I hadn't dropped the bags and turned tail and run into the house, forcing them to acknowledge the problem and cancel their trip and spend David's hard-earned vacation time checking Cameron into the loony bin.

Which would require me to leave the house.

After they left, I went to my room and shut the blinds and read. And watched Nick at Nite. And *didn't* look at college catalogs. Why bother?

That was four weeks ago. At first, I made myself go outside. Just a little a day, never realizing that one day I just wouldn't be able to leave at all. The first week, I actually did mow the backyard, which is so small you can do it with a Weed Eater and is surrounded by a high wooden fence so it feels safe, or safer than the front yard at least.

But after that, I couldn't stay out that long, so I just opened the window and watched the grass grow.

And now the door has been closed for a week.

And the telephone is ringing.

I know who it is, who it always is. Mom calls every day at noon. To update me on David's mother's condition. (They'd decided to stay longer.) To find out how I'm doing. Do I have enough money? Am I eating all right? I know Mom must suspect something, but she can't acknowledge it. Because acknowledging it would mean doing something about it. So our conversations go like this:

Mom: Go to the grocery store, Cam. I know you don't like to move off the sofa lately, but pizza three times a day isn't a balanced diet.

Me: Yeah, okay.

Mom: Call Mrs. Wilson if you need anything.

Me: Yeah, okay.

Mom: She said she was over, but you didn't answer the door. Were you out?

Me: Yeah.

Mom: Are you sure you're okay, honey?

Me: Yeah, okay.

And then the silence.

Sometimes I don't answer so they'll think I'm out. But today I pick up the phone.

"Some friend," says the voice on the other end.

It's Sean, back from camp.

"What's your problem?" Although I know.

"My problem? Oh, just the seven or eight letters I sent with no answer from my best friend."

"Sorry."

"I'll bet."

"First you manage to talk your mom out of sending you with me. Then you don't even answer my letters."

"Sorry. I've been busy. Did you send many letters?"

"You know I did. Seven or eight."

"I only got two."

Which is true. That's how many I got before I called the post office to ask them to stop the mail. The mailbox is at the top of the driveway.

"Really?" Sean's voice is uncertain.

"Yeah," I say, warming to the lie. I have to tell so many. "Yeah, only two, and they just got here a few days ago. I figured you didn't have time to write me. Then when I got them, I knew you'd be home soon."

Stop. You're talking too much. One secret of a good lie: no unnecessary details.

But Sean doesn't notice. "Oh. I should have figured it was something like that. What's with the lawn?"

"Oh, you know. I'll do it right before they come home."

Sean laughs. "When's that?"

"Another week."

"We should get together," Sean says. "I want to tell you about this girl I met at camp. Melinda. We . . . well, we did some stuff."

"That's great. Great." *Will I ever have a girlfriend?*

"Can you come over?"

His voice sounds far away. I can barely hear it. My heart is pounding. My face is flushed. My skin feels tight around my temples, and I haven't even gone anywhere. I am definitely nuts.

Before my throat closes completely, I say, "No, not today. I'm sick. Flu."

"Oh." Sean sounds bummed. "Tomorrow, maybe."

"Maybe." Holding the phone away from my face, sure Sean can hear the shallowness of my breathing. "Probably not. I'm pretty sick. Could be contagious. I wouldn't want you to get it."

And before he can say anything else, I say I'm going to sleep and hang up.

And sit on the sofa and stare at the door, which has now been closed for a week.

When Sean calls the next day, I let the machine pick up. That afternoon, he comes and knocks on the door, but I don't answer.

The day after, it's his mom's voice. Do I need anything from Walgreens?

I pick up. "That's okay, Mrs. Wilson. I have everything. Thanks."

"You just get better, sugar. Sean's looking forward to seeing you. You sure you don't need anything?"

"No. I'm just tired. I think it needs to run its course."

"You rest, honey." I can tell she's glad to be off the hook. She's done her duty.

I start to say goodbye, then think of something else. "You won't tell my mom I'm sick, will you? I don't want them to worry."

"All right, sugar. Let me know if you need anything." She hangs up.

I hang up too and stare at the door, which has been closed for nine days now.

I want to go to Sean's house. I really do. Or at least have him over here. Only problem is, I just can't open the door.

I realize I haven't even walked close to it in three days.

I stand.

"It's just a door," I whisper.

I stare at it. Wood, stained the color Mom had called honey when we refinished it two summers ago. Before. Mom and I had stripped off the white paint using the finest-grained sandpaper so as not to wear down the hand-carved flowers on the panel under the knob.

"Be a shame to throw it out," Mom had said. "They don't make them like this anymore."

I'd agreed and sanded it—gently—making certain to remove every last white fleck, then stained it and changed the old chrome doorknob for one of shining brass. And that afternoon, I'd gone to the park with Wyatt and Sean to jump off the bridge and into the canal—which wasn't strictly legal but was fun.

And now I stare at the door until its golden flowers and golden knob blur together in a golden haze and wonder how I was ever so stupid—or so brave—to do something like that.

I start across the room.

One step.

Two.

Keeping my attention on other things, not looking at the door, not daring to look. Mom's collection of porcelain vases is to my right: red, yellow, blue, all a blur of painted flowers. The table with its photography books spread out to the left, full of pictures of places I'll never go.

And between them, the door.

The closed door.

I step closer.

I'm okay until I think of opening it. Then fear grips me like a hot, wet hand, cutting off my breath, constricting my throat. My heart is pounding, pounding, pounding— my head is hot and floating someplace far away.

And the door is there. The door is there. The door is there. The door is there.

I reach for it.

A wave of panic seizes me like the ocean, grasping,

engulfing, immersing me. What's out there is too terrible to contemplate.

I turn and run, sending one of Mom's vases crashing into the door.

I retreat to my room and lie on my bed, squeezing my pillow to my face.

I am definitely nuts.

The door has been closed for eleven days now.

The broken vase pieces still lie in front of it. I don't want to get that close.

Sean has stopped calling. His last message on my answering machine was: "Fine. Don't answer my calls. You never want to do anything, and now you won't even talk. I guess Wyatt was right. You *are* a snob."

Click.

I tell myself it doesn't matter, but it does.

Sean, Wyatt, and I had been best friends. Sean lived next door, and we'd known each other forever, or at least since he'd moved in, when he was four. He and his mother knocked on the door—yeah, that door—carrying Happy Meal toys by way of an introduction.

"My mother said we can be best friends," Sean had said. So we were. And when we'd started junior high and were both on the baseball team, it had just seemed natural to include Wyatt too because he was the pitcher.

We'd started ninth grade at Pine Ridge High with big

hopes. Varsity by sophomore year, district champs by junior. College scholarships or maybe an invite to play in the pros. But tryouts were still ahead of us, and guys in high school sure looked huge.

And one day, something happened in the cafeteria.

It was a Friday. I remember because they always serve spaghetti on Fridays. Three guys, seniors—or maybe sophomores who'd been held back a lot—stood over us. They were all big, and one was huge. I'd never seen them before.

"You're in our seats," the biggest guy growled.

I stopped eating, food hanging out of my mouth, and just stared. Sean didn't say anything either.

But Wyatt said, "Don't see your name on them."

"You don't, huh?" another guy said.

"Nope." Wyatt was acting the way he did on the mound, this false bravado I'd always admired—but not today. I was beyond scared and ready to move. Seats weren't worth it.

But Wyatt kept going. "We've sat here every day this month."

"Well, today's the last day," the big guy said.

"Who says?"

"I do." He put his hand into my spaghetti, raked up a handful, and shoved it in Wyatt's face.

I didn't—couldn't—move.

At that point, one of the narcs the school got to patrol the cafeteria came over—a short guy, smaller than the guys he was supposed to protect us against. While Wyatt spat out used spaghetti, the narc put his hand on the big guy's elbow.

"What you think you're doing, boy?"

The big guy took a swing at the narc. The others joined in. Wyatt, Sean, and I managed to clear out while someone went for the principal.

So it was over. But I still remembered. Relived it, really.

Over the weekend, everything was fine. The three of us went to the batting cage at Tropical Park, and I was at my best. "We're definitely making the team this year," I'd said.

But Monday, when I got to the cafeteria doors, I could not go in.

The left double door is kept locked, so everyone has to go through the right. I'd come from the English wing, while Wyatt and Sean had come from science. So we usually met inside. Except, that Monday, my feet felt rooted to the floor.

"Move it." Someone behind me.

But I couldn't. I could not move forward. I had the strangest feeling, like I wasn't real anymore but was floating above myself, watching. That feeling gave way to terror. I wanted to run back, but people crowded against me from behind. The only way out was in . . . and I was not going in.

I couldn't breathe. I couldn't *breathe.* I was trembling, choking, and then I felt numb. Behind me, people were yelling, pushing. I needed them away from me. They were suffocating me, making me die. I wanted to run, but they pressed against me, killing me, killing me. I had to get away. I had to get away. But I could not move forward. I could not move at all.

"What's the matter with you, man?" Through my head's pounding, I heard Wyatt's voice. "What the hell's your problem?" He shoved me away from the door.

"Don't be so rough with him." Sean's voice.

"He's freaking out."

Then Wyatt was off me, and Sean was there. The feelings began to subside.

"What's wrong, man?" Sean whispered.

"I just . . . I can't go in. I can't go in there."

"Those guys are gone, Cam. They got suspended, expelled maybe. It was just a one-time thing."

"I know." And I did, which is what made it so crazy. Yet I knew if I went in, I'd pee my pants or get beat up. At best, I'd be subjected to total humiliation. At worst, I'd get hurt. "Look, can't we just get something from the roach coach?"

Wyatt grumbled but followed Sean and me to the roach coach. It's this truck with a horn that plays *"La Cucaracha"* that comes to the back of the school where they have Driver's Ed.

So, for the next few months, we got roach-coach sandwiches. And everything was fine.

Except some mornings, when I'd stand at the front entrance, looking at the *Home of the Cobras* mural and the trophy case, I'd feel it. That same raw terror that had come through me that first day in the cafeteria. It washed over me like a wave. The urge to run. I fought it. I told myself that nothing like that had happened before or since, that I wasn't one of those victim kids, that I could take care of myself. But when I walked inside the school, my head hurt and I felt sick. And always, I was afraid that what happened that day in the cafeteria doorway would happen again. That I'd be trapped, unable to move forward, with everyone staring at me. That I'd look stupid or maybe die.

And one day, I didn't even get that far. I stood, looking at the school, at the people driving up or walking, slogging backpacks. And I had to leave. I had to leave.

I turned around and went home, hammers beating inside my chest. The feeling subsided.

"What's the matter, honey?" Mom asked when I showed up on the front doorstep.

"I don't feel well," I said. "My stomach . . ."

"Oh, we'll get you some ginger ale." Mom led me in and closed the door.

I could tell she didn't mind having me there. So the next day, it just seemed easier to say I was still sick.

And the next day.

The day after that was Saturday. I woke up feeling fine and met Wyatt and Sean at the park to practice. Tryouts were coming up. Sunday, same thing. I thought I was over it.

But on Monday, I woke, thinking—no, *knowing*—I couldn't go.

I went down to breakfast in my pajamas.

"What's this about?" David asked.

"I can't go to school. I don't feel well."

"What do you mean? You felt fine yesterday."

"You can't miss any more school," Mom said.

"This is getting ridiculous," David said to Mom. "He has to go."

"I can't." Even just sitting there, I could feel my throat closing up, my heart pounding. And beneath it, the knowledge that if I went to school, I'd get beat up or humiliated. I didn't know what, exactly, couldn't put it into words they would understand.

"I can't go," I repeated, knowing I sounded deranged.

It finally ended with my getting dressed, David standing over me. Then Mom drove me to school.

When we got there, I couldn't get out of the car. Finally Mom took me home.

That's when I started homeschooling.

"Who can blame him?" Mom had told David. "Looking at those kids, I wouldn't want to go either. It's not like when we were in school. The boys look like hoodlums and the girls all dress like that Britney Spears. A kid could get shot just for showing up."

David said he guessed it didn't matter. He'd be at work anyway.

For a while, it was only school. I'd still gone to Sean's and Wyatt's houses and played ball and did all the things I'd done before. Around here, you can walk into town to do stuff. Then it was only Sean's house and car trips to town with Mom and David.

And now it's just the door.

The door, which has been closed for fourteen days now.

And the telephone is ringing.

I consider ignoring it. There's nothing to say. But on the tenth ring, I answer.

It's Mom.

"Where were you, sweetheart?"

"Oh." I try to make my voice sound casual. "Just met Sean and Wy over at Circle K."

"You're not buying groceries at Circle K, are you? It's twice as expensive."

"No, we just got a Slush Puppie. I'm not stupid, you know." *But you are if you believe me.*

"Oh, okay." Mom's voice relaxes. "Good news. David's mother is doing much better. We'll be home in a few days."

A few days?

Hearing my silence, Mom goes on. "Not very long. We'll be home next Thursday."

Next Thursday is eight more days.

"Are you okay, Cam?"

No! Come back! But I know she can't. If David wants to stay, Mom will stay. She doesn't like to rock the boat.

The whole homeschooling thing has been bad enough. So I say, "I'm fine. Fine. It's just . . . Sean's here. He was talking too, so I couldn't hear you."

"Oh. Anyway, we'll be home next Thursday. Okay?"

"Fine, Mom. Fine."

"We'll send you more money."

"Fine."

I let the receiver slip from my hands and into its cradle. I sit back, staring at the door.

The door stares back at me.

It's been closed for fourteen days now.

My mother will be gone eight more.

Sean is somewhere, having a great time with Wyatt. They'd made varsity last spring. I have no friends, no life.

And another problem: my food supply is running low.

I walk to the kitchen. The garbage is brimming, and three black bags of it swell in the corner. I know what's inside: boxes and cans, all the packages from everything I've eaten in the past month. Empty boxes of frozen chicken nuggets, empty bags of frozen ravioli, crushed Cap'n Crunch boxes, cartons from eggs and cans from soup and tins from nuts, jars from spaghetti sauce, wrappers from cheese, and cartons from pizza, and lots and lots of those funny white containers that Chinese food comes in.

I'd been careful to shove any leftovers down the garbage disposal. But even so, with five weeks of trash, the kitchen is starting to smell.

More than starting, actually.

I walk to the cupboard to take inventory.

Three cake mixes that need eggs to bake.

A jar of applesauce.

Two cans of clams.

Cornmeal.

Oil.

A jar of artichokes.

Green beans (which I hate).

In the refrigerator, there's:

No eggs.

No milk.

No cold cuts.

No cheese.

A lemon.

And half a can of chili mac.

I'd started stockpiling food when Mom and David announced their trip, stowing stuff away like a squirrel to make certain I had enough.

"Where's that ziti I bought?" Mom would ask.

Or "I could have sworn I had macaroni and cheese."

And I'd always shrug, though what she was looking for was in the back of my closet, behind my unused catcher's mask and glove.

But even in my squirrel-like efforts, I'd assumed I'd be able to order in.

At first I had. But now the door has been closed for two weeks.

I look out the front window. Mangoes, dozens of them, hang from trees and litter the lawn.

But my fear is between us.

Beyond the trees is the street, and beyond the street is the town with grocery stores and McDonald's and friends and school and everyone I know and the life I once had and wanted.

But my fear is between us.

I look closer, just across the trees, at Sean's house. There's a light in his window, and I can see him moving around. He's alone, like I'm alone. He was my best friend. I want to see him. Talk to him. He'll think I'm crazy, but I want to say, *Help me, Sean. Help me.* But my fear is between us.

My fear, and the closed door.

The door is there.

The door is there.

The door is there.

I start toward it, then stop.

I stare at the doorknob.

God, I don't want to die.

I don't want to be crazy, either.

And mostly, I don't want to be alone, trapped in this house, starving for more than food. I want my life back. I want to play baseball.

I know what I have to do.

I take another step and wait for the wave to engulf me.

It does.

My face is hot, then cold.

I'm sweating; my heart pounds.

The door is there.

The door is there.

Another step.

The door is there.

Another.

The door is there.

I feel dizzy, like I'm drowning, like I'm going under for the last time.

Still, I stumble forward, stepping on shards of Mom's vase. They crumble underfoot.

The door is there.

My heart is pounding, pumping in my ears, in my throat, threatening to choke me.

I reach for the door.

I touch it.

I hold the dead-bolt lock with all my strength as the waves engulf me, as everything goes neon and purple, then black.

I flip the lock, then run, panicked, back to the sofa.

I collapse, winded, sweating. I sit a long time, listening to my breath and staring at the door, the unlocked door.

It's almost an hour later before I can pick up the phone and dial Sean's number.

But I know I have to tell someone. I have to get out of here.

■ ■ ■

ABOUT THE AUTHOR

Alex Flinn's three young adult novels—*Breathing Underwater, Breaking Point,* and *Nothing to Lose*—have earned an awesome number of honors, including a Top Ten Best Book for Young Adults and a Quick Pick by the American Library Association, a Top Ten Youth Mystery by *Booklist,* and Best Young Adult Book of the Year by Barnes & Noble, as well as winning a Black-Eyed Susan Book Award and being nominated to numerous state book award lists.

Although Alex Flinn is not agoraphobic like the character in "The Door," her closest friend, Debbie [not her real name], started showing early signs of that terrible fear shortly after they graduated from college. After a traumatic experience, Debbie "started refusing to drive or be driven on the expressway," says Flinn. "Then she began to avoid the highway, too. Or anyplace with which she was unfamiliar. Although she was looking for a job, ironically, in mental health counseling, she refused to enter what she termed 'bad neighborhoods.' In the space of a year, her world shrank to a few miles."

Sometime after that, Alex Flinn read Susan Isaacs's novel *Almost Paradise,* in which the main character struggles with agoraphobia.

"The book hit me like a fist," she says. "This is where Debbie had been heading, had she not sought treatment early."

With that as background, Alex Flinn says this about her story: "I wrote the first draft in a single sitting. I felt rooted to my seat at my local coffee bar. I could not leave. I ended up eating a vile, overpriced tuna melt in order to avoid leaving my seat and the story. I felt trapped, like Cameron, and had to write my way out."

. . .

For most people it's just a street.
But for Robert, it's . . .

Calle de Muerte

. . . . .

Ron Koertge

I'm shooting baskets in the driveway of my house, faking Kobe and Shaq and LeBron right out of their jockstraps, hitting from everywhere. Really. I'm not imagining that last part. I'm hot—getting all the bounces. Lay-ups and hooks. Jumpers. Three-pointers from downtown and beyond. Nothing but net.

What do I look like to the average guy driving past? A kid in a tank top with a hot hand, that's what. Perfectly normal. Maybe a little scrawny, but lean and mean for sixteen. No tattoos, but what Mom calls a Hoover special, which means I make my hair stand straight up like a vacuum cleaner is doing its best to suck it right off my scalp. It gets on her nerves, so I like it a lot.

I also like this fantasy, so I put a couple of girls in that average guy's back seat. Him being nice and all and taking his kid and her friend to the mall. And they pay zero attention to him because they're in their girl-world, but they see me out there. They watch me sink a couple. They lean close enough to almost touch, and they whisper. Nice things. About me.

Then I miss a shot, and the ball takes a crazy bounce, rolls right down the driveway and into the street.

Oh, man. Tell me that didn't happen!

Kobe and Shaq knock me down and stand on my head. The girls roll their eyes and laugh—*pathetic.* Because the best I can do is get to the curb. The ball is seven, maybe eight feet away. Waiting. Taunting. I just stare at it. And start to sweat. Not good, clean working-out sweat, either. But nasty stuff. The kind that seems like it could eat through my clothes. The kind that'd probably look green and glow in the dark.

I backtrack to the garage. My mom outlines every tool we own. You know the kind of outline I mean, right? Like the chalk around the body on crime shows. But in Magic Marker. Right up there on the pegboard: pipe wrench, claw hammer, ball peen hammer, coping saw, spade, et cetera. She hates for things to be in—get this word—"disarray." She actually said that. She's a nice enough mom and I get my better-than-average vocabulary from just being around her, but "disarray"? About a workshop in the garage? Get serious.

Anyway, I go in there, get the rake (leaving its little outline for the crime-lab guys), trudge down the drive, and take a swipe at the ball. Wouldn't you know it. Just out of reach. I feel like that Tantalus guy in the Greek myths who could almost get to the grapes but not quite.

I'm leaning, lunging at the ball, nearly getting it, coming within, I swear to God, inches. So close. Just another millimeter. Then I slip off the curb.

Which freaks me out completely. I make a little choked sound, a whimper, not even a groan but a groan-ette. And all but collapse. The rake is gone. Forget the rake. I'm windmilling both arms just to keep my balance because I do not under any circumstances want to pitch forward.

Which almost happens. Then I feel the curb on the backs of my ankles and go over backward. Gratefully collapse. End up flat on my ass but not in the street.

That's the point. I don't care where I am or how stupid I look, I am somewhere besides there.

"You okay?"

For a minute I think it's the street talking to me. Ragging on me. Daring me. Going *mano a mano,* though in this case it would be *hombre a calle. Contra,* actually: "man against street."

But it's not the concrete talking. It's a girl. A girl in a blue tank top. A girl with lots of hair. A strong girl: big shoulders, smooth brown arms. And all of that, all of her, in a wheelchair. Though not one of those clunky ones, not a chair-on-wheels so that she could just get around. No way. This one's a lot zippier. Streamlined. Lots of chrome. A real ride. And she's not just in it, not plopped there, not confined. But part of it. Part girl, part device.

I get up and brush myself off. I'm calmer already. Panic is like that—it comes and it goes. No way is this the first time, either. I know the drill.

And I've got my back to the street now, away from that concrete scab on the earth that separates me, in a way, from everything.

"I'm fine."

Isn't that what guys say? 1. *It's just the jugular, I'll be fine.* 2. *That is a sword sticking out of my ear, but I can hear you perfectly. I'm totally fine.* 3. *I know the car has me pinned to the tree and if it backs away I'll be in two pieces, but I'm actually fine. Let's talk about you.*

"Want me to get your ball?" she asks.

"That's okay. It's an old one." What am I going to do, tell her the truth? She'll think I'm nuts.

"I'll get it," she says, "anyway."

"Just leave it!"

"Will you relax?"

This is hard to watch. Hard for me. Humiliating. Because she fearlessly veers off the sidewalk, scoops the ball into her lap, retrieves the rake, tosses that onto the grass, then gets back up over the curb with a move that shows she's about ten times stronger than I am and flips me the ball.

I rocket it back at her. "I told you I didn't want this thing!"

She rolls up the driveway, dribbles a couple of times, and makes a neat little bank shot. "I don't see why not," she says. "It's a perfectly good ball."

And she's gone.

All of which makes me feel like talking to somebody. (Not *sharing*, okay? I hate that word; it reminds me of half a sandwich.) Dad knows what my problem is, but he treats it the way he does aches and pains, i.e., don't pay any attention to them and they'll go away. My mom knows but she doesn't understand. Do you get the difference? She knows what's wrong with me and can spell it. She's seen the symptoms and read about them. But she hasn't been there. It hasn't happened to her. She's never been that scared. She's never panicked and had her heart attacked. She's never stood on a curb and trembled and felt like she was going to pee her pants. She's never thrown up and passed out.

But I know people who have. People like me. Scared of the same thing or different things. There's even a kind of online scene: The Fobes, they call themselves. And inside that a pecking order. A hierarchy. From somebody who calls himself Luxor (he says he's afraid of everything, including his computer, and claims to be sweating bullets every time he boots it up) down to Starving Tarpon, who I cannot take seriously ever since we had this little online conversation:

Me:	Poetry. You're afraid of poetry?
	I'd love to just be afraid of poetry.
Him:	Think again, man. Poetry is everywhere.
	Like if I hear somebody say, "I know a place
	that's neat to eat," I just start shaking.
Me:	That's not even poetry. It's just rhyme.
Him:	Rhyme is bad. A real poem could kill me.

There's a lot of drama among the Fobes. Lots of weird one-upmanship. My mom hates anybody's holier-than-thou attitude. Well, I'm suspicious of more-scared-than-thou. Worse-off-than-thou.

But who else am I going to talk to?

It's what, two nights later, maybe? And I see her in the library. Wheelchair Girl. Who is probably eighteen, a couple of years older than I am.

She's obviously doing research on something because books are piled up all around her. My mom, the teacher, would call it a caricature of scholarship because it's a little too picturesque—a wall of books to her left; a leaning tower of them to her right; three or four sprawled in front of her; plus some downloaded printouts, their light pages moving in the air conditioning.

When she lays down her pen and starts to roll backward, I tell her, "I'll get it for you."

"Pardon me?"

"Whatever you want. I'll get it for you. You got my ball, remember? Not to mention my rake."

"Oh, it's you, Mr. Personality."

I look down at the table. "Yeah, sorry about that."

"Apology accepted, but I'm fine."

"C'mon, that's what I always say when I'm not. A little quid pro quo never hurt anybody."

She thinks that over. "All right. There's some stuff at the printer. Under O.S. But don't throw it at me like you did that ball."

When I retrieve the pages, I make it a point to hand them to her super-carefully. Then I ask, "What does O.S. stand for?"

"Olivia Sharpe." Her hand comes out. Her gloved hand. Partly gloved, anyway. All five fingers are exposed. It's interesting that she wears those even when she's sitting still. Primed for a getaway, maybe?

"Robert Delgado." We shake and she shows me how strong she is. Which is really strong, and not just for a girl, either. "Uh, about yesterday . . ."

She glances up; her eyebrows are perfect. "Yeah?"

"I've got a little problem."

She's still wearing her shades, even though we're inside. Prescriptions, probably, but with yellow lenses. The kind shooters wear. Marksmen. "Mrs. Martinez told me. She didn't know the word for it, but Google did: you're agyrophobic, right? That can't be easy."

Damn it! "Mrs. Martinez. What a *metiche.*"

She reaches for her pencil. "What's *metiche*? I would think *chismosa.*"

"*Chismosa*'s okay, because she gossips. *Metiche* means poking into things. Mrs. Martinez is both."

Somebody not far away makes the classic *shhh* sound.

Olivia whispers, "Give me five minutes and we'll go outside? I need a break."

I take out my math book and do a few problems in my head, but all I can think about is how I wish I hadn't thrown that ball at her. To her, actually, but still. She's nice, she's pretty, and she doesn't seem totally freaked out that I'm afraid of a little asphalt and concrete.

Olivia and I settle by the stone lions. We're at the little local library—not the big one uptown—so it's very residential. Cars go past. People with their dogs and those appetizing little plastic bags.

This was her idea, but she doesn't say anything. So I do. "What were you reading in there?"

"Porn."

That stops me. But her grin is ambiguous.

"If," she says, "porn is something unattainable that you long for."

I shake my head to show I'm following, but barely.

"There's all this stuff on the Net about people like me with spinal cord injuries. Stem-cell research, stuff like that. A breakthrough is always a decade away. But I can't help myself; I read it anyway."

Olivia takes a Clif Bar out of a deep bag slung on the side of her chair, tears it open with her teeth, takes a big bite, and says, "What's it like around here, anyway?"

I can tell she doesn't want to talk about stem cells anymore. "Well, Highland Park isn't what it used to be. Ten years ago, there weren't any galleries or coffee shops. No lofts with assigned parking. And almost everybody spoke Spanish."

"Your folks are Hispanic."

"Just my dad."

"What does he do?"

"Sells cars."

"Is he the Delgado on TV?"

I wince. "With the cowboy hat. Yeah."

"What a sweet deal, though: a different car every day if you want."

"Unless they're parked on the other side of the street."

A couple of kids race by on their Big Wheels. Kid one veers down the disabled-access part of the curb and shoots across both lanes. Kid two stands up, straddles the big gaudy toy. Waves.

"That makes me wistful," Olivia says.

"I know what you mean." I do, too: she wants to put two feet on the ground. I want to cross without thinking.

"What happened?" I point to her chair.

"A horse. Just like Chris Reeve. Only he was really unlucky. How about you?"

"It wasn't too bad at first, but it got worse. I just . . . little by little didn't want to . . . uh, you know, step out there. And then I pretty much couldn't."

"Let's hope they have the prom at your house."

That makes me grin. I like how she says it. I like the edge it has. I like her. Not in, you know, a girl-boy way. I just like her.

"I can get places," I assure her. "It's just kind of a pain. My folks take me. Riding in a car is no sweat. I'm not amaxophobic, too."

"So do your friends pick you up if you go someplace special?"

"When they do."

"Which means they usually don't?"

I just nod.

"Tell me about it. After the accident," she says, "my pals were, like, 'We'll call you.' 'We'll go out.' 'Nothing's changed.' Like hell nothing's changed." Eyes right at mine. On mine. Into them. Then out again. "Or maybe I'd be like them if things were the other way around. I hope not."

"I think the U-turn was a little too much for my friends."

She puzzles that for a second, then brightens. "Oh, to get you—"

"Yeah. Right in front of the movie or the restaurant or wherever. And if whoever's driving is too cranky to bother with a U-turn, I have to cross like in a herd. With people all around me. Or I can close my eyes and run. Which means I'd definitely be the first guy to go on *Elimidate*."

"You watch trash TV?"

"Once in a while."

"Me, too. The chicks are such skanks, I can feel superior. I might be in a wheelchair, but I don't stick my tongue down just anybody's throat. Have you got a girlfriend?"

"Did the word *skank* remind you of the kind of girl who might like me?"

She doesn't miss a beat. "I had a boyfriend. Until that horse fell on me. Then it was like I'd broken my lips, too. Not one lousy kiss afterward. Not in the hospital, not in rehab. *Nada*." It's warm out, so she lifts all her hair and hopes for a breeze. A guy with a little white cart comes our way selling pineapple, mango, and papaya on a stick. "So," she says, "we know my sad story. What made you phobic?"

"You don't kid around, do you?"

"Meaning?"

"I just, you know, don't talk about this to people who haven't been through it or who aren't getting paid to listen."

"Don't tell me if you don't want to."

"It's embarrassing. Don't you think it's embarrassing? And pathetic to just come right out and say I'm afraid of the street. No wonder I like the big Latin word. I tell somebody in plain English and they're like, *Are you kidding?*"

"You're in, what—tenth grade?"

"Eleventh."

She shakes her head. "A living hell as I remember, and I was mobile then. But not as bad as eighth, where if you fart once, you're the Gas Man for life. Do they call you names?"

"Retard."

"Lovely. C'mon. Let's get something to eat."

I follow her down the ramp, and we hail the guy with the cart. I let her talk to him because I'm pretty sure she wants to practice her Spanish. Without asking, she gets me pineapple, which is what I would've asked for. Her papaya is the red kind from Mexico. She uses it to point.

"So there it is. *Calle de muerte.*" She gives it a little spooky tremolo. " 'Street of death.' "

I glance at Avenue 60, then glance away. "It's not that bad. And I know I don't have to cross this one, so it doesn't bother me."

"And you've seen a shrink."

"Sure. He said the usual stuff: wanting to control my environment, the unconscious protecting itself, childhood trauma—"

"What kind of childhood trauma?"

"I don't know. Or at least I don't remember. And neither do my folks."

"So no blue ball in the street, no little Robert running blindly for it, no screeching brakes and terrified-then-really-angry parents."

I shake my head. "Maybe it just runs in the family. My grandfather was kind of compulsive: oatmeal every morning at eight o'clock sharp, clean socks at noon, nothing yellow in his lunch. That kind of thing."

"I guess you've seen those ads on the Net."

I crank my voice up a notch or two and wave both arms around wildly. "'Cured in fifteen minutes!!!' 'Call now: operators are waiting.'" Then back to normal. "Talk about something unattainable that you long for!"

"It doesn't work?"

I take a bite of pineapple; she takes a bite of papaya. We chew together.

"I don't know," I say finally. "Maybe. Not for me, though. Mom did send for a book once and we did what it said."

Olivia leans forward. "And?"

"It was basically replacing negative associations with positive ones in, you know, your mind."

Olivia arches the stick her papaya was on right into the trash bin.

"Do you shoot hoops?" I ask.

She nods. "I could give you points and still kick your

ass, but don't change the subject. Did you have negative associations?"

"Not that I know of. But for positive ones, I imagined Britt Pretrykowski in the middle of the street, smiling and motioning for me to come on out and she'd tell me a secret."

"And Ms. Pretrykowski is a local goddess, I take it."

"For sure."

"What happened?"

"She got hit by an imaginary bus, which made me guilty and phobic."

Olivia's got a nice laugh. "How about acclimatization?"

"You did do your homework. Yeah, I remember acclimatization."

"So?"

"I just . . . I don't know. I'm lazy maybe. It just takes so long."

"And you're otherwise occupied doing what, exactly?"

"I know, I know. You're right."

She looks at her watch, one of those that tells the time on Mars or nine thousand feet under the water.

"The first day I was in rehab," she says, "I knew it was either get with the program or collect little glass animals and feel sorry for myself. You're not collecting little glass animals, are you?"

There's a part of me that wants to tell her to mind her own business. But not as big as the part that says, "I should try again."

"I'll help if you want."

"Like how?"

"I didn't," she says, "go through rehab alone. Why should you have to acclimatize alone? I'll just bring a couple of pom-poms and sit where you won't throw up on me."

"Why are you doing this?"

She shrugs. "We're neighbors."

"Neighbors borrow hammers and then don't bring them back. This is like beyond neighbors or neighborness, or neighborality, or whatever that word is."

"Believe me, Robert. This isn't charity. I just moved here, just started community college. I don't know a soul. *And* you could teach me a little Spanish."

"Well, sure—when I'm not throwing up or passed out."

"I'll take my chances." Out comes her hand. "When do we start?"

I look at her. "Saturday morning?"

She nods and then she's gone. "See you then" thrown over her shoulder like a scarf.

Once Mom picks me up from the library and I'm home that night, I don't instant-message anybody or drop into a chat room or do anything with the fobe-site except eavesdrop. No way do I want to tell them about Olivia. I can hear it now: *Is she cute? Is she hot? In a wheelchair? Are you kidding, man?*

There's a new guy claiming to be caligynephobic, which means he's afraid of beautiful women. Like he's surrounded by those twenty-four hours a day. Otherwise it's the same motley crew. It makes me wonder who some of these people would be if they weren't phobic. Dr. Lee once asked me that: "Who would you be if you weren't afraid of crossing the street?" My answer? "The guy on the other side with the chicken!"

And some of us get there, too. I like success stories. People who improve. Are less afraid. Who handle their phobias rather than the phobias handling them. Are more than their dilemmas. Who if they don't get cured at least get better.

And what do these people get for logging on with good news? Criticism and doubt. Ridicule and suspicion. Why? Are the fobes phobic about being unphobic? What's the Latin for that?

Putting on my pajamas, I started thinking about Olivia. How does she get into bed? Does somebody help her?

I wiggle my toes, something she can't do. Then I glance at my computer. Think about my Internet pals again. The ones I don't want to talk to.

I remember this one night. Somebody who calls himself Paperboy was bragging about this cool girl he'd met. The others started in on him. Working away. Undermining him. Ended up with Sonic Daddy telling Paperboy that she wasn't his type. Wasn't good enough for him.

So there's a guy afraid of string giving bad advice to another guy afraid of fish. Who goes there—friend or fobe?

By Saturday morning, I'm having second thoughts. What's so terrific across the street, anyway? Just more of the same—more houses and people, more malls and doctors' offices, more coffins and chandeliers.

Not really those last two. They're across more than the street. They're across many streets. But let's say I wanted a coffin or a chandelier. Just get on the phone. Whip out the old credit card. Someone delivers it right to the door. Or somebody could drive me. What's so bad about that?

Except I wouldn't get to see Olivia.

I dress better than usual: polished shoes, new turquoise polo shirt. And slacks, not khakis. Slacks with a crease.

Dressed for success, even if success means only getting one foot off the curb and out into the insubstantial air. Just that. Just hovering over the gutter because the gutter isn't the street, okay? It's the gutter. If it was the street, it'd be called the street. But it's not. It's the gutter and I'm not gutterphobic.

My parents sleep in. The neighborhood is quiet, the laws of coming and going still in neutral. I think if the day is a book, then this is the first page.

Down the walk I go, my parents' walk, the one that intersects the public walk running east and west, the real sidewalk I could turn onto and go as far as the end of the block, then left, left again in a few minutes, another left, and I'm back where I started.

No way. Then I see Olivia, even though we didn't say what time we'd start. "I was thinking," she says without even a hello, "that you're kind of like Rapunzel. Everybody has to come to you."

"Rapunzel's problem was vertical. Mine's horizontal."

"True." She takes in my outfit. "You look nice."

"I thought maybe I could dazzle the street with my masculine allure."

"I'm sure that'll work." She rolls backward a foot or two. Makes room for me to pass on the way to the . . . well, you know. "Let's see," she says, "what you've got."

Even though *acclimatization* means getting used to something little by little, I stride right out, reject the beckoning east and west of it all, and head for the curb. Right for it. Immediately I start to pant. My lungs feel like little duffels with almost no room left at the top. The sweat starts in my hair, of all things. Not under my arms or at the small of my back. Oh, no. But in my hair. Where it gathers, collects, assembles, meets others of its kind, and starts down my forehead. Breakfast (eggs, toast, milk) that seemed like such a good idea at the time, now curdles in my stomach. My heart feels huge and hot.

How wide is that street, anyway? Now that I'm close,

it looks enormous. Like a river. But a river I don't have to wallow in. Don't have to swim across. Today, anyway, all I have to do is put a toe in. One lousy toe.

When I'm almost there, I stop like I've hit a wall. And I wish it was a wall, because I'd lean on it; I'm that woozy. I remember trying this with Mom. How it felt. How she cried. No wonder I gave up.

"Push me, Robert."

Somehow Olivia's in front of me. I look at the shiny black handgrips on the back of her chair.

"I thought you were just going to wave pom-poms."

"Push," she says.

"God, Olivia."

She points. "Just ease me down to where the you-know-what starts." She turns and looks back up at me. "And don't let go or I'll shoot right out there, get run over by a Ford F-150, and then you'll really feel bad because I'm not just some positive association like Britt Pretrykowski."

I stop. Glance down. Sweat pours from my hairline. "I don't know, Olivia. My heart's already beating fast."

"So?"

"My legs are weak."

"You're talking to the wrong person about that, *amigo*. Mine are numb. C'mon. Let's say hi to the thoroughfare."

"The what?"

"The thoroughfare. The boulevard."

"Synonyms don't help."

"The path maybe?"

"Oh, man."

"Lean on the chair."

"I'm already leaning on the chair. And I've got my eyes closed."

"Good idea. Just a little farther."

I feel the wheelchair drop off the curb. I hear a car whoosh by. "Are we there?" I ask.

"I am. You're still on the grass. Come on in, the gutter's fine."

I stick my foot out and wave it a couple of times like Hans the Wonder Horse counting to two. Then pitch forward. Is a curb eight inches high? Twelve? It feels like I'm tumbling into the void.

I'm leaning, bent over. Wiping at my eyes with one hand. "I'm sweating buckets."

"So back up."

"What?"

"Pull me back on the curb. Then you'll feel better."

I lean instead. Move forward a little. "Now where am I?"

"We are there, my friend. We are in the street."

"Seriously?"

"For sure. Another nine thousand increments like this and we are all the way across."

"Well, that's ridiculous."

"No!" And she's gone. Pulls herself right out of my hands. She negotiates a neat little wheelie that puts her face-to-face with me because I've pretty much collapsed by then. "No, it's not either ridiculous."

I gasp. "Really. Then why am I sitting on the curb with my head between my knees?"

She reaches for me, puts one strong hand in my thick hair. Tugs a little, pulls me toward her. "What's Spanish for 'You did really well'?"

"*Hiciste* . . ." I can't finish till I take a deep breath. *"Hiciste bien."*

"And it's true. You know what the normaloids say, don't you?"

I look up at her and shake my head.

"One step at a time." She shoves me. It's playful but she means business.

I stand up. The street might as well be the Mississippi. A thought that makes me so wobbly I sit back down. "Son of a bitch." I find Olivia and focus on her. "Is it okay if I swear?"

She shrugs. "I'm not your mother."

"Do you want to meet her?"

Olivia looks at me over the tops of her yellow sunglasses. "Interesting transition."

I brush at my slacks. "I was looking at the house last night. There's just two steps in back. Dad and I can help you up those. Otherwise there's plenty of room to get through the doors, and any rugs that get in the way we can move. Basically there's nowhere you can't go."

"Your mom's okay with this?"

"And Dad. I, you know, talked about you at dinner. A little."

"So do I want to meet them?"

"Right." I look over my shoulder. It's not the Mississippi. It's just a street. "I mean we're neighbors. *Vecinos,* right?"

She rolls the word around in her mouth before she smiles. She has a big smile. A nice one. Which she should use more. "Yeah," she says, "I guess we are at that."

■ ■ ■

ABOUT THE AUTHOR

Poet, short-story writer, novelist, writing teacher—Ron Koertge can be humorous, deadly serious, and always entertaining. From the publication of his first novel for young adults, *Where the Kissing Never Stops,* to his most recent *Margaux with an X,* this California writer seems to get better with every book. Among his publications are *The Arizona Kid* (which the American Library Association singled out as one of the 100 Best of the Best Books for Young Adults published between 1967 and 1992); *The Harmony Arms* (a YALSA Popular Paperback for Young Adults); *Tiger, Tiger Burning Bright* (a Judy Lopez Memorial Award Honor Book as well as a *Bulletin of the Center for Children's Books* Blue Ribbon Book); *Stoner & Spaz* (a Michigan Thumbs Up! Honor

Book and winner of the PEN West Prize for Children's Writing); and two novels in verse: *The Brimstone Journals* (a YALSA Best Book for Young Adults and winner of the Kentucky Bluegrass Award) and *Shakespeare Bats Cleanup* (a *Voice of Youth Advocates* Top Shelf Fiction Selection for middle schools).

His short stories have appeared in such diverse anthologies as *Destination Unexpected, On the Fringe, 13, Tomorrowland, Rush Hour: Sin, Twelve Shots,* and *What a Song Can Do.*

As to why he chose to write about agyrophobia, Ron Koertge says: "I stay close to home a lot, anyway, so I was interested in what it might be like to pretty much have to stay in the neighborhood." In an effort to be as realistic as possible, he says, "I even pretended to be agyrophobic in order to feel what those constraints might be like. Made it a lot harder to get to the racetrack, that's for sure. And cranked my frustration level way up!"

. . .

Deenie is sure she doesn't have any unhealthy fears.
She just wants to be . . .

Thin

· · · · ·

Joan Bauer

I step on the bathroom scale, hoping for good news. I do
this every morning, but this morning the news is grim.
I've gained two pounds—*impossible*! I've been so careful
about what I eat, unlike last week, when I fell apart due
to monumental stress and two major episodes of intense
rejection. I had pulled myself together, too, being a person of extreme determination who can banish weight
quickly—but now this scale is just taunting me and I feel
like a swollen mass of excess weight. To make things
worse, I have school all day, so I can't work out until the
afternoon, and despite chugging water to rid myself of

the hated weight, despite having a single piece of sugar-free gum for breakfast and a plain salad without dressing for lunch, I still feel like a brazen blimp to the point that I just want to hide in a dark hallway and not be seen by anyone. I can't focus in class because I picture my thighs enlarging and my stomach distending until I get as round as that huge Snoopy balloon in the Macy's Thanksgiving Day Parade. I imagine my entire body blowing up beyond oblivion and sailing over the treetops while people say, "Whatever became of Deenie . . . ?" and I'm trying to shout down that I'm *here*. Someone, *please* come and get me. Something awful has happened. It is intensely difficult to focus on Shakespeare's last four sonnets, as I am supposed to in English Lit, when these episodes occur.

I say *episodes* because it's not the first time this has happened, *but* that doesn't mean there's something wrong with me. It's not like I'm anorexic—I maintain a reasonable weight. It's not like I'm bulimic, although I did take those laxatives last month—but *only twice*. I'm the first to admit that I have to work hard to keep my weight under control. I have to work with heart and courage to fine-tune my body because of the stupefying pressure on females to always, always look great. The mirror being held up today is pretty hard to compete with—all these perfect women on TV, in magazines, on the Internet. All of that reflects back, you know. Anyone who says it doesn't lives in deepest, darkest denial.

So please don't tell me about how all these images

floating at us are computerized, engineered, and cropped. Are we turning into a society of totally retouched human beings who are composites of someone's imagination? Absolutely. But look, the bar's been set—that's how it is—and I for one am not going to lose ground like my mother, who doesn't diet or exercise. She's gained forty pounds since my dad left us to live with Chloe, this really thin, younger woman he met on an airplane and according to him, "The sparks just flew." I'm never going to get fat. I don't have time for all the guilt and all the concern and how my mother wants me to see this therapist. I don't have time for the school counselor who wants to talk to me. I don't have time for people who can't share my vision.

Something happened yesterday at lunch. It was enough of a thing that I got kind of scared. I was trying to eat this salad and I had this choking sensation and my throat closed up and then I had a full-out panic attack where I couldn't catch my breath. I had to sit with my head between my knees for at least ten minutes with all my friends giving first-aid opinions:

"Breath deep, Deenie."

"Let yourself relax."

"Let your body go limp."

"Breathe into this paper bag."

I did the deep breathing, inhaling slowly, but my heart was beating so fast I couldn't relax. I inhaled through my nose, I exhaled through my mouth, making a soft, relaxing *whoosh* sound that is supposed to bring inner peace, which it almost did. I tried not to focus on anything except the normal progression of breathing. I closed my eyes and tried to close my ears to the sounds around me, which are significant in a cafeteria, but the smells of second-rate food just came at me, assailing my senses. I tried to focus on the sound of my breathing, and after a few minutes I was just fine and I stood up and told everyone to stop looking so worried. I said this as Jessica Chen walked by and announced in her ultimate voice of self-righteousness, "Deenie, that used to happen to me, too." I really didn't want her amateur diagnosis, okay? So I went to class and felt fine, except for my legs feeling a little rubbery, which was understandable given the cafeteria incident, and my hands being a little shaky, which happens now and then. I don't know why.

I've perfected these isometric exercises that I can do when I have to sit still, and in doing them I can work my legs and exercise my abs, which really need adjustment; I can tighten my butt, which needs major firming. There's simply no excuse to stop moving or exercising as long as you're awake. I've been doing these exercises in school for months now and made the supreme mistake of merely mentioning this to Shondra O'Neil, who declared that I had some kind of phobia—"an unhealthy fear of ever getting fat," she decreed—like trying to stay in shape and being focused on serious exercise is unhealthy. Shondra is probably going to become one of those caustic advice therapists on the radio. She'll be perfect—she has no heart and diagnoses people in a heartbeat.

Jonathan's afraid of success.

Delia is too self-absorbed.

Crawley is overcome by fear—his father is ruling his life.

Shondra announces these things with venomous authority as if she has a total bead on the truth, and the crazy thing is, people listen. Mostly, I think, because they're afraid of her. Shondra goes off on these psychological tirades and everyone around her goes mute, or as Jessica used to call it, Shondraphobic.

But saying I have a phobia—that is just an intense, pathetic joke, because it's not like I see a spider and can't sleep for days. It's not like I'm afraid of going out in public. I'm not afraid of heights or small enclosed spaces (as evidenced by my minuscule bedroom).

I suppose if I could change anything, it would be that I'd not be so nervous. I'd like to not feel so guilty when I eat an occasional treat. I'd like to stop imagining how calories are affixing themselves to my thighs and abdomen. I'd like to stop seeing myself as an obese monster that needs to be lifted onto the street by a crane because I can't fit through the front door. I'd like to just walk down the halls at school and not wonder how many calories I'm burning every single minute.

When I was a little girl, I never thought about these things—I'd just go out and play, get dirty, and eat more cookies than I should. I'm not sure what happened, not that it's a problem, you understand. Not that I'm some phobic personality who lives in the shadows, constantly washing my hands like an obsessive-compulsive raccoon.

Despite all of this, I am dragging myself to the gym, embracing full-throttle self-discipline. I eat one-eighth of a protein-packed low-carb energy bar (34 calories), guzzle water from my no-drip exercise bottle, and walk quickly past the Comfort Bakery that has, I swear, fans to blow the aroma of their mammoth-size cinnamon rolls with candied walnuts and thick icing onto the street. I am almost struck dumb by temptation, but these are the moments that separate the strong from the weak. I embrace my life goals of never, ever gaining weight, of toning every muscle in my body to become all that it can be, which, trust me, is a lot. I let the real voice within me speak.

Think, Deenie, how very much you want to have flat abs and a perfect body.

Think how that will change your life.

I'm halfway across the street when a car screeches to a stop in front of me. The driver honks long to make a point, *way* too long.

Okay, I didn't see the green light. I've been kind of scattered lately. I scream, *"Thanks for not killing me!"* which really gets this guy going and he's shouting that maybe next time I won't be so lucky, and he finishes the threat with his middle finger extended, to which I shriek, *"Get a life, you bozo!"*

Now he's honking and swearing all the way down the

street and everyone is looking at me; I feel exhaustion just crashing in. I should have kept my mouth shut. I know. I've been popping off at people lately. I don't know why.

I walk into the gym and try to get psyched about exercising, because the Total Power Workout is not for the disengaged. Lately, I don't feel like exercising. I feel tired all the time. I don't know why. I shake negativity from my mind. Exhaustion is a state of mind that must be overcome.

I head into the locker room and try to still my heart, which is beating hard due to the brazen bozo encounter. Basically, I want to go home and take a nap, but I can't. I won't. My mother says I have to give myself permission to relax. She doesn't understand. I splash cold water on my face, grab a towel, and shake off the memory of my once and former best friend, Jessica Chen, who used to work out with me. That's *used to,* past tense. She wrote me this horrific letter saying she was so worried about me and how, in her unprofessional opinion, I was obsessing about exercise and fear of fat and that I had really gone over the edge.

Getting angry sucks energy from a person's core. I toss it off and march out to face the Body Beast, a turbocharged stair climber with upper body weight extensions, shimmering before me in brushed metal. *Fully loaded,* my father would say. At least I think he would. I haven't seen him in a long time.

I get on the stepper and set the timer for sixty minutes. I don't believe in starting slow. I'm sucking in my abs, using all the strength I've got. I'm doing full arm tense/release motions with the pulleys to heighten body sculpting. I visualize my body taking sugars out of my bloodstream and converting them to energy. I picture those two un-wanted pounds falling off of me and never coming back.

I turn up my extreme workout drum CD; the rhythm pounds away so that I have to go faster and faster—stopping is not an option. The drums won't let me stop. It doesn't matter how I feel, doesn't matter what time it is.

I have to exercise.

I have to move.

I have to make sure that every muscle group in my body is doing something productive.

Sculpt those abs.

Firm those thighs.

I am moving toward the pain and burn, which is the goal in the war against weight, which is why, and I've tried to explain to my mother, I keep going even when it hurts.

The Beast shows respect by emitting a little roaring sound, which means I've gone thirty minutes.

Keep going.

Make the exercise do more.

I choreograph my breathing—exhale during exer-tion, inhale as I return to starting position.

Pushing, pulling, stepping, breathing.

I am one with the Beast and this is all I know, except I'm not exactly one with the machine today. I'm just struggling to keep up. I'd like to ratchet down, but the thought of that makes me step faster and harder. My right knee has that twinge of pain again, which is probably messing up my focus. I feel the burn creep across my face and neck, coming through my legs and arms, which are straining to go farther and tougher than ever before.

I close my eyes and feel the burn, which means my fat is sizzling off. I think of how Jessica would shout YES when that happened. I tell you, she was *extreme*—was, that is, until she started seeing that therapist who told her she was overdoing it, getting phobic, and she needed to cut back. Fine, so she did. And then she started telling me there's more to life, too much exercise is bad for you, and how she learned to give herself permission to be, to rest, and how she felt *so* much better and blah, blah, blah.

The muscle in my neck is beginning to spasm, but I ignore that because I know the truth. If I keep going, I'll stop focusing on it. If I keep going, everything will be all right. If I keep going, keep moving, keep stretching, keep pushing, keep lifting, then I will be . . .

What? What will I be?

I shake off that thought. Non-answers are like sabotage. I just want to achieve total body perfection. It's not like I'm getting completely reshaped by plastic surgery. I'm not spending zillions of dollars on clothes. I'm just looking to be a highly trained physical specimen. The Beast emits another roar. Sixty minutes now—I push on for ten more.

*   *   *

I am in the stretching room doing two hundred side ab crunches (that's two hundred per side).

One hundred eighty-nine.

One hundred ninety.

My stomach muscles are shrieking. Good. Ten more. I strain to finish.

One hundred ninety-one.

I make two hundred and fall back down, feeling like all the energy has been let out of my feet and is pooled up on the floor like a plumbing leak. I close my eyes and lie flat to stretch out my back, which has been just a little sore lately, but then I've been accelerating things. The back always takes a while to catch up with super-human pace.

I point my toes out and stretch my arms back, going for a full body stretch. I hold it for a long time, feeling every tendon tighten. It is not as much fun exercising alone.

Whenever I get off the stair climber, I always feel strange—I'm much more confident when I'm exercising than when I'm not. This fear starts creeping in that I didn't go long enough, and now that I've stopped, I'm not burning enough calories, and if I eat anything, I'll gain weight.

Once my mother said to me, "Deenie, what would happen if you just stop for a while?"

Part of me wanted to laugh when she said that because

the thought of ever stopping was absurd. The other part of me wanted to cry. I didn't know how to tell her.

I can't stop, Mom.

If I do, I just know that something bad will happen.

I should have taken the bus home instead of walking. I'm so tired and shaky. I don't know why. I buy an orange juice and drink the whole thing—160 calories. It makes me feel a little better, but I hate wimping out and taking in calories I just don't need.

I get home and head upstairs to weigh myself. I know weight fluctuates throughout the day and I should weigh myself at the same time every day, but I just can't help it. I'm standing at the bathroom door, looking for the light. I feel so lightheaded; my legs feel like rubber. I hear my mom calling, "Deenie, is that you?"

I try to hold on to the wall to steady myself.

"Deenie?" Mom shouts.

That's the last thing I hear.

It's not a bad cut on my head, honest. It's just a little blood; the bump is mostly black and blue from hitting the sink on my way down to bond with the scale, which, I suppose, is darkly comic under the circumstances.

"Sit down," Mom says. "And breathe deeply."

I'm getting sick of people telling me how to breathe.

"I'm getting ice, honey. Will you be all right?"

I nod. "I'm okay," I say. "I'm okay." I don't feel dizzy anymore. I just feel stupid.

Mom comes back upset. "No ice. We forgot to fill the trays." She runs the cold water—sticks her finger in, waiting for frigid. She wets a towel. "Hold this on your head."

I hold it.

"How's that head feel?" Mom asks.

"Like I fell in the bathroom and hit my head on the sink."

Mom looks down at me with her soft brown eyes. "I need to ask you a very important question."

I squirm. I don't feel like dealing with very important questions right now.

"What are you afraid of, Deenie?"

I don't know what to say. Usually Mom asks different kinds of very important questions.

How do you feel about your dad leaving?

How are you now that you and Jessica aren't friends much anymore?

"I'm afraid of the usual stuff, you know."

She just looks at me and that's all it takes. I start to cry. "How do I answer that question, Mother? *What would you say if I asked you what you're afraid of?*"

She leans forward. "I'd say I'm afraid for you, Deenie. I'm afraid you're hyperfocusing on weight since your dad left and—"

"Look, you want the scale, Mom? Take the scale. I don't want to see it anymore. I don't have to step on it. I don't have to drive myself crazy."

"Deenie, I want to help you."

I pick up the bathroom scale. *"You want to help me? Hide the scale. No matter what I say. Don't give it back to me. I'm serious."*

I'm standing in the bathroom where the scale used to be and I am here to tell you, this is agony. I didn't realize how much I need to monitor my weight until I couldn't, but I'm not going to admit that to my mother and get her more worried than she already is. I'm not going to tell her how I feel like I'm being smothered by this fear regarding my weight and how I simply, simply have to step on that scale. It's too hard to know it's somewhere in the apartment.

I hear my mom in the shower, so I begin to ransack her bedroom, which is where she usually hides things. I'm looking through drawers, throwing clothes on the floor. I head for the closet, shove things aside, get up on a chair. I need the scale. I *need* it. I can't go outside and see people; I cannot face the world without knowing how much I weigh.

I find it at the top of Mom's closet covered over by my old baby blankets. I put it on the floor and step on it. That's when Mom comes into the room; she's in her bathrobe with a towel on her head. She stands there for a long time.

"Well," she says finally, eyeing the scale. "You found it."

I make a joke. "It's where you hide the Halloween candy."

She looks at the mess of clothes on the floor.

I'm breaking out in a sweat. "Look, Mom, I'm just used to monitoring my weight, okay? It's hard to break the habit."

Mom kneels down and picks up the sweaters I threw on the floor. I hate it when she goes silent and hurt.

"I'm sorry, I was just trying to find it, and I didn't want to bother you, and . . ." My voice sounds high and shrill.

"And do you feel better now that you found it?"

My mouth feels chalky because the answer is no. I feel worse. I don't want to be imprisoned by a stupid scale.

The towel falls off her head. She doesn't care. "What is going to make you feel better, Deenie?"

"I don't know what you mean."

"What is going to help you get off this?"

"I'm not *on* something, Mom."

"Something's got ahold of you that isn't right."

"I just wanted to know how much I weighed."

"What are you afraid of, honey?"

Tears pour out of me. Mom comes over to put her arms around me, but I don't want comfort, okay?

I look out the window, weeping uncontrollably as all the fear spills out of me. "I'm afraid if I stop, I'll shut down. I'm afraid if I stop, I'll be like a helium balloon that loses air and just lies on the ground. I'm afraid I won't be interesting. I'm afraid I'll get fat. I'm afraid of being afraid and I don't think about it nearly as much when I'm working out intensely. I'm afraid I'll be too emotional and people won't want to be with me. I'm afraid Dad won't want to be with me."

Mom's close to tears. "Oh, Deenie . . ."

"I'm afraid I can't stop. I'm afraid I'm stuck in this thing and I'm going to exercise myself into some kind of break-down. I'm afraid I'm sick. . . . I'm afraid there's really something wrong with me that no one can fix."

"Okay," Mom says in a shaky voice. "We start here and now. You know the first step out of any problem?" I shake my head and blow my nose. "Admitting you have one."

I cover my face. Finally I say, "Jessica's got a therapist for this."

"Call her, Deenie." Mom kneels down and puts a phone in my hand.

I look at the phone then close my eyes. "I can't. We're not—"

"Call her," Mom says.

Call my once and former best friend. Let's just make this day a complete disaster. I look at Mom and she looks back at me like she did when Dad walked out and she said somehow we were going to be all right. Somehow we were going to get through this together.

I dial the number. How many times have I dialed Jessica's number?

"*Hel*-lo."

Jessica always answers like this.

This is so hard. "Hi. It's—"

"Deenie!"

I smile. "Yeah."

"Are you okay?"

Such a simple question. All these tears hit my eyes.

"Am I okay? No, I'm not. I think—I think I need the name of that therapist you're seeing because . . ." I'm all-out crying now, but Jessica's heard me cry on the phone before.

"You're going to like her, Deenie." She gives me the name and number. I write it down; hold the paper tight. "Tell me how it goes, okay?"

I nod through tears.

"I'll see you at school tomorrow, okay?" Jessica says. "Call her *now*, Deenie."

"Okay . . ."

I hang up, sigh deeply, and dial.

■ ■ ■

ABOUT THE AUTHOR

You're probably familiar with Joan Bauer because of one or more of her always humorous and touching novels, which include the Delacorte Prize–winning *Squashed,* the *Los Angeles Times* Book Prize–winning *Rules of the Road,* and the Newbery Honor Book

Hope Was Here, as well as *Thwonk, Backwater, Sticks,* and *Stand Tall.* Or you may have run across one of her short stories in anthologies such as *On the Fringe, Love and Sex, Necessary Noise, Shelf Life, Trapped, From One Experience to Another,* or *Rush Hour: Sin.* She is one of the most admired writers in the business, and one of the most delightful people you could ever meet.

When asked what prompted her to write about being thin, Joan Bauer said, "I think that there is impossible pressure these days for females to look perfect. I actually lost fifty pounds when I was nineteen and I've managed to keep it off, but I remember the struggle of that. I always wanted to be thin, and, I'll admit, sometimes I could be pretty crazy about it. I wanted to show a girl who had just hit bottom and was forced to see that she had a problem."

Joan Bauer says this was a very emotional story to write "because, in some ways, I could feel her crumbling, and yet she was still defensive and confused." Reverting to humor, as she often does, Joan confesses: "I still need to watch my weight because, honestly, inside me is a five-hundred-pound woman screaming to get out. I *love* to eat and I just have to watch it, but at times I've also gotten carried away—eating not nearly enough, almost following a punishing diet. And if I'm really honest, I think that fear fueled a great deal of that. But enough! I'm going to get a chocolate doughnut."

. . .

James is trying to cope with his fear of string as best he can.
But then he falls in love with . . .

D'arcy

. . . . .

Angela Johnson

I used to think it was just a nightmare. I always woke up shaking.

Back in the day, when I was about five, there were superheroes on my walls and I woke up in my racecar bed. I guess I'd yell out in my dream 'cause there would be my pops standing beside the bed with a worried look on his face.

He'd stay awhile and talk as the sun came up. But finally he'd have to go take a shower. And since I wasn't shaking anymore, I'd walk down the hall to the kitchen.

I'd get the cereal bowls and spoons out. Breakfast then was anything crunchy, sweet, and poured out of a box.

Oh, yeah, I'd sat there in my Underoos while Pops played oldies from the '80s on the radio and remembered the nightmare. The day we had that strawberry cereal with marshmallows was the first time my "thing" showed up. Damn, sometimes you got to wonder about stuff.

I mean, I was just this little happy dweebie kid playing with my buds, watching too much TV, and eating too much sugar. Then there was this "thing." Nothing was ever the same after that. Nothing.

Now I wake up to Mos Def on my CD player and my favorite poster of an armed bear chasing hunters through the woods. I sleep on a futon now 'cause I don't have so far to fall when I roll out during the nightmare. See, I still have the "thing." Maybe one day it will go away.

Maybe.

The day it all happened, I was yelling at Pops to get to the table for breakfast. We were having his favorite: garbage-can home-fries with onions, garlic, tomatoes, cheese, green peppers, and bacon.

"Yo, Pops, get in here before I throw it all away."

He came in looking tired. He'd been at the office late the night before. I worried about him. I wish he had a normal job like most people. I mean it's not like I'm ashamed or anything about what he does. I guess I wished he had a job like my friends' parents. You know—something respectable like a factory job or working in a store. I guess he can't help that his dad would only send him to college if he became a lawyer. I ain't mad at him. He's still my pops.

"Mmmm. This is good. What's up with you, J?"

I stand by the fridge drinking coffee and wiping the counter with the new dishtowel. There'd been a mistake a few days ago when I sent Pops out to get new ones and he'd gotten the fringed kind. I was just getting over that one. He had to cut all the little strings off while I went into the bathroom and sweated it out.

It was building up. All of it. It used to be just thread and thread coming undone from hems. And maybe fringe on things and skinny ropes and the ends of helium balloons. Now it's worse. Man, it's pretty exhausting to be string phobic. It's not something you tell people about 'cause usually they laugh and call you a liar. Or they just laugh so hard, they can't call you anything.

Anyway—there'd been a few incidents throughout my life that are better left unsaid. Well, maybe I'll tell you.

There was the camp incident with the knot-tying. Pops had to drive two hundred miles to bring me home. Those Boy Scouts and their ropes and string.

There was the bad time when my old babysitter kept me at her house and we found out too late that she'd lived through the Depression and she had a thing about saving string—everywhere in her house.

I could go on . . . but I won't.

"Nothing. Just gonna hang out today. Hector doesn't need me to do any stocking today, so I think I'll call up Cole and roam."

"Sounds good to me. I'm in court all day, so my cell won't be on. Leave a message if you need anything."

Then he was gone, and it had already started to get way hot like July in Cleveland did. I called Cole's house and her little sister, Deniesha, picked up the phone, speaking in a bad French accent. I laughed and she went and got Cole.

"What up, J?"

"I'm not working today. Come over and pick me up."

"I got Deniesha all day. She'll have to come with."

"That's cool."

So it was on. But as I was pulling on my LeBron T-shirt, who knew what was coming? If I'd known, I would have fought the flies off me from the hammock all day—even with the big hole in it that trapped you when you tried to get out.

Cole's car had been her uncle's, before that his son's. Now it was what Cole called "comfortable" and I call a piece of junk that looked good. But it was still a better piece of junk than I had—which was nothing 'cause the old man wasn't going to let me drive until I was eighteen. I was embarrassed but knew he had his reasons so I didn't sweat him.

So the first thing I say as I get in the car, while pushing Deniesha over the seat into the back is, "Let's drive through Metroparks."

Deniesha straightens one of her fairy wings that got twisted when she was pushed in the back and says, "You just want to go looking for that girl who smiles all the time and—"

Cole swings around and hits her with the pillow she sits on to drive.

I throw Cole a dirty look, then act like I'm interested in the shrubs by the garage while the kid laughs herself sick in the back of the car.

Okay. I told you that something had happened to change everything. Well, that something was D'arcy Sykes. I love D'arcy Sykes.

D'arcy Sykes is good. She loves animals and children (even Deniesha). She volunteers at the hospital and animal shelter. She writes letters to political detainees in foreign prisons and wouldn't litter to save her own life. D'arcy Sykes is everything I ever wanted. D'arcy Sykes never has a bad word to say about anybody and smells like apples.

Everybody knows her and likes her.

She says hi to me in school, and her locker is four away

from mine. She's a goddess, and the rest of the world should throw fruit or rose petals or things that grow on bushes and trees before her.

The park's pretty crowded with soccer kids and baseball teams stretched for miles. Cole drives through and I wave when I see somebody I know. D'arcy was volunteering somewhere in the park. I thought she was probably picking up litter or working in the animal preserve or something. I had been looking for her all summer but hadn't found her.

Cole calls our drives to the park DHs (D'arcy Hunts).

It was getting close to noon and we still hadn't found her—again—and Deniesha was starting to whine about being hungry and having to pee. So Cole parks the car (the Metroparks go on for miles) and we all get out to find a vendor. Deniesha runs off to go to the bathroom nearby, but when she doesn't come back after ten minutes, Cole gets nervous. We are just getting off the bench when Deniesha runs into view, eating a hot dog, like some kind of deranged fairy in overalls.

She spots us and runs to us.

"Where have you been? I was just coming to look for you when—"

"I found her, J. I found D'arcy over there."

She points toward a long wooden building over by a pond.

So now my mouth gets dry and my hands start to shake 'cause I know after a summer of looking for her with Cole, I'm not going to get out of talking to her. Cole would probably make me walk the five miles back home if I didn't.

She puts her arm around Deniesha.

"Good kid. There's an ice cream in it for you."

I smile at her, a little sick to my stomach, and start to walk across the grass toward the building. It's like a quest now.

I feel better as I get closer. I can slay dragons. I can cross crocodile-filled moats. I can scale treacherous mountains and climb peaks so high I'd need oxygen. I could cross the Shoreway at rush hour. . . .

So when I'm finally turning the corner of the building, Deniesha grabs my hand and pulls me the rest of the way.

Then . . . I almost pass out. There's my beautiful D'arcy with about ten women, sitting in the shade of a big tree with looms in front of them and baskets of yarn beside them.

Deniesha jumps up and down, and D'arcy gets up from her loom and comes over to me and smiles.

"Deniesha tells me you're joining our class. Isn't this wonderful, ladies? This is James. He goes to my school and he'll be the first young man we've ever had in weaving class."

*   *   *

I really can't remember anything much after that except when D'arcy smiles, the beads on her braids shimmer and the sun gets brighter.

Cole takes me by the hand and walks me back to the car, telling me all the time about how Deniesha doesn't know about the phobia and wouldn't understand if she did. Cole's a good friend and I have to remember that it's probably better if I don't see Deniesha for a few years 'cause who knows what I'd do to those fairy wings.

I have the nightmare again and this time I can't wake up in time. I must scream real loud 'cause Pops is standing over my futon looking more tired than ever.

Love is stupid.

Love is hard.

Love makes you do things that you would never do for anyone.

Love sucks, just like a fear of string and anything that looks like string does.

But I love D'arcy and I'm going to weave.

Love is stupid.

* * *

It's a sick world we live in when they have stores full of nothing but yarn. . . .

Wool Gathering is off Pearl Road in a strip mall with Hot Dogs Hot Dogs and something called Sips & Snips. Cole says it's a beauty parlor–bar. I don't see how that could be legal, but what do I know? I'm just standing in front of the wool place with my face pressed to the glass and my eyes closed. I've taken my allergy medicine, so I'm almost in a coma and probably won't go into shock when I walk through the door. Cole is holding the list of things I'll need to start weaving with D'arcy next week.

I focus on the colors of the carpet when we walk into Wool Gathering. I focus on the nice lady who introduces herself as Peggy—or Mary or Delores—I don't know which. I focus on how I'm gonna need new tennis shoes and how if she saw it in a fashion magazine, Cole would wear fried eggs on her feet and body.

Cole talks and buys. She could have done it without me in the store, but she said I had to come. She said pretty soon I'd have to touch the yarn. Then where would I be?

I say under my breath, "Hopefully near a hospital bed with some sedatives." And I hoped she hadn't heard me 'cause she can get pretty pissy about courage. She has it and I don't—about yarn.

I manage to get out of Wool Gathering only hyperventilating a little, with just a touch of hives.

I say to myself, "It's a phobia, it's a phobia—you can't help it. . . ."

Love hurts, and stings.

In my nightmares, I'm always reliving the accident over and over. It goes like this. There's spinning and a loud crash after the car flies in the air. Then my mom and me lay upside down for what seems like hours until someone finds us at the bottom of the ravine. The car's flipped over. There are tags everywhere. I know why they are there. My mom was taking the tags to her friend who's judging some sort of show. Strings are hanging from the tags, and because neither of us can move in the car, we are covered in them.

I yell myself awake and imagine I see D'arcy at my bedroom door. I smile, lie down again, and go back to sleep. I don't even see Pops back out of the room.

Cole drops me off in the parking lot near the shelter house. Deniesha is not with us today. Cole says something about a play date, but I'm pretty sure she's trying to keep us apart for now.

I get out of the car with my bag of yarn, which I haven't touched yet, and my other weaving tools.

I head toward the shelter house.

I head toward D'arcy.

I head toward sheer terror.

I head toward D'arcy.

I head toward panic, hyperventilating and dry-mouthed.

D'arcy.

Complete terror.

D'arcy.

Queasiness.

D'arcy.

D'arcy. D'arcy of the shimmering braids and the golden light around her.

Well, I couldn't use the wool anyway after I was sick all over it. How I even carried it that far toward the shelter house is still a mystery. And it's a good thing Cole is my friend and had my back. She'd waited in the parking lot for me and asked if I needed a Coke when I walked back to the car like a zombie.

Love hurts.

And hurts.

And hurts.

I've been hanging around the house for the last couple of weeks. I'm still afraid of strings and yarn, and my pops still looks tired. When Cole came by, we didn't talk about much at all—until yesterday, when she asked if I wanted to go for a ride. I finally said yes. And even though Deniesha was sitting on the hood in a new pair of wings and late July in Cleveland is steaming, I was ready to live again.

It's all over now, and I try not to obsess over what happened. What's really important is that I have Cole, and as long as there isn't a textile mill moving into the neighborhood, everything is going to be okay.

■　■　■

ABOUT THE AUTHOR

Born in Tuskegee, Alabama, and a graduate of Kent State University, Angela Johnson is an amazingly versatile author who is as comfortable writing poems and short stories as she is writing picture books for children and novels for teenagers. Along with other awards, three of her books have received the Coretta Scott King Award—her first novel, *Toning the Sweep,* in 1994; *Heaven* in 1999; and *The First Part Last* in 2004. Two of her other books have been Coretta Scott King Honor Books—*The Other Side: Shorter Poems* and *When I Am Old with You. The First Part Last,* in fact, was one of the most honored books of 2004, winning not only the Coretta Scott King Award but also the Michael L. Printz Award for Excellence in Young Adult Literature and being chosen as one of the Top Ten Best Books for Young Adults by the American Library Association. Among her other publications are *Songs of Faith, A Cool Midnight, Running Back to Ludie, Looking for Red,* a collection of short stories called *Gone from Home: Short*

Takes, and the picture books *I Dream of Trains* and *Just Like Josh Gibson.*

In 2003 she was awarded a John D. and Catherine T. MacArthur Foundation grant given to people who have shown "extraordinary originality and dedication to their creative pursuits and a marked capacity for self-direction."

When asked why she chose to write about a fear of string, she said she could imagine herself having various other phobias, so writing about those "wouldn't have been too much of a stretch for me." She chose string "because for me it's the strangest one."

And what does Angela Johnson want readers to remember most about her? "That I've always tried to be a good gardener, and though I fail miserably, I keep trying."

. . .

Why should anybody be afraid of an ordinary house cat?
For Randy, it's a matter of . . .

Claws and Effect

· · · · ·

David Lubar

She has a great personality.

That's supposed to be what they say about a girl when she isn't real pretty or smart or anything. But that's nonsense. Phoebe has a great personality. And she's more than just pretty. She's stunning. Especially when she smiles. She's the first girl who's ever paid any attention to me.

I'm amazed she likes me because, let's face it, I can't even pretend to have a great personality. I'm a total geekazoid. If I was in a movie, I'd be the guy in the group who doesn't get any lines. If it was a horror movie, I'd be the first to die. Maybe even during the opening titles. If it was a comedy, I'd be the one who accidentally drinks a whole bottle of laxative or gets locked out of his house when he isn't wearing any clothes.

But, somehow, Phoebe's my girlfriend. And I'm not in a horror movie or a comedy—I'm in my junior year at Crescent High, which was pretty much the same thing until she came along and turned it into a romance. Me and her. Phoebe and Randy. It would all be perfect, except Phoebe lives with Johnny Depp.

I learned that the hard way the first time I walked her home from school. We'd been hanging out together for a couple weeks, mostly in the school library, and then at lunch. That's where we'd met—right in the library— when we'd reached for the same book on coral reefs.

"Go ahead," I'd said, stepping back from the shelf.

"No, you take it," she'd said. "Do you have a report to do?"

"Nope. I was just going to read it for fun." Oh, God— I winced at the sound of that. The words marked me as a total geek. Who reads science books for fun? I could feel my face getting hot.

"So was I." She smiled at me. I never thought braces could look so cute.

I found out Phoebe was as passionate about oceanography as I was. And I discovered it's not hard to talk to a girl, even a stunning girl, if you both love the same thing.

We met last Saturday at the mall for a movie. I guess that was our first real date. We held hands, and she rested her head against my shoulder. It was nice. Monday, she suggested that I should offer to walk her home. Which I did, since I can take a hint after I've been hit over the head with it three or four times.

We chatted about small stuff for most of the walk, but there was one big thing I needed to know. With a couple minor exceptions, I'm a rational guy. I believe there's an order and a meaning to the universe. Stuff usually makes sense. The thing I needed to know was, *Why me?*

I couldn't come right out and ask it that way. I had to sort of creep up on the subject. "You date much?" I asked.

"Not really."

"But you're so . . ." I searched for a word that would sum things up without sounding wrong. *Hot? Awesome? Wonderful? Out of my league?*

Phoebe saved me by answering the question I was trying to ask. "A lot of guys are scared of smart girls," she said.

"You're kidding."

She shook her head. "Nope. No joke. I guess they feel threatened or something. But not you, Randy. You don't seem to be scared of anything. Not even smart girls."

"That, I can handle," I said.

"Besides, you're kind of cute. Especially when you smile."

I grinned at her, but kept my mouth shut so I wouldn't say anything stupid.

"Want to come in?" she asked when we reached her house.

"Yeah."

As I walked up the porch, I noticed a flap at the bottom of the front door. My stomach felt like I'd just yanked my belt a notch tighter than normal.

"You have pets?" I asked, trying to keep my voice from quavering, which was already hard enough, since I was a bit nervous about going over to her house.

"A cat," Phoebe said.

I froze on the steps. Years ago, we'd had a cat. I was too young to remember what exactly I did or what exactly he did, but I still have enough scars on the back of my hand to make it look like I went through some sort of tribal rite of passage.

"Want to meet him? He's a total sweety-puss." Phoebe glanced around, then called, "Here, Johnny! Come here, boy."

Don't panic. Okay, she has a cat. But it's not a problem. Cats don't come when you call them.

"Johnny!" she called again. "Johnny Depp!"

"I'm sure he'll show up later," I said. Everything would be okay. Cute little Johnny was out somewhere in the neighborhood, chewing the head off of a sparrow or ripping the intestines from a chipmunk. My own stomach began to wriggle free of my esophagus and slide back down to where it belonged.

"Oh, there he is," Phoebe said. "Come here, sweetie."

Oh, yeah. There he was. One of those scrawny gray beasts. Thin and mean-looking. An outdoor cat. That meant he had claws. And teeth. I glanced at the row of small white dots on the side of my right hand near my thumb. Healed tooth marks. My intestines felt like they'd been overfilled with warm water.

Phoebe knelt and held out her hand. But instead of going up to her, the creature padded toward me. As I stood there, trying to decide what to do, he put both his front paws on my leg, stretched, and extended his claws. He stared at me with the cold eyes of a serial killer.

I wanted to scream and run. So did my last meal. I knew Phoebe expected me to say, "Nice kitty," and pet him. But there was no way I could touch that animal.

"Isn't he just so adorable?" she asked.

I nodded. *Not to me.*

She bent down and snatched him up. His claws pulled at my pants leg like evil Velcro, but she finally yanked him free. My knee tingled from the feel of those tiny needles.

"Come on. Let's go in." She jiggled the cat. "Johnny can keep us company."

Johnny was still staring at me.

"Oh, God—I just remembered. I have to water my aunt."

"What?"

"Water my aunt's plants," I said. "She's away. I promised I'd water her plants. And I forgot. If they die, it will just kill her. She's like ninety-seven. Sorry, gotta go."

I turned and fled.

Behind me, I heard Phoebe call, "Come back here."

I almost stopped. But then she said, "You come back here, Johnny Depp."

Oh, crap. I didn't even look to see whether he was chasing after me. It was supposed to be dogs who did that. And bears. Not cats. But I wasn't taking any chances. I ran as hard as I could for three blocks. Which isn't easy when your lungs have turned to concrete.

Stupid cats. I can't stand them. Not even on TV. They completely creep me out. Every time I see one, I can just imagine it leaping on my face and biting. Or shredding my eyes with its claws. I know that isn't rational, but I can't help it.

"Are the plants okay?"

"What?"

"Your aunt's plants?"

"Oh, yeah. I got there just in time."

We'd met, as usual, outside the school. Phoebe didn't seem to be upset that I'd rushed away. I decided the best strategy to avoid another encounter with Johnny Depp was to invite Phoebe to my place. "Want to come over after school?"

"Sure. I'd love to."

Wow. A month ago, I would have been terrified of asking a girl to my house. But, facing a much more tangible fear, I'd hardly thought about what I was doing before I spoke. Maybe terror wasn't so bad when it pushed you to do other things you were just slightly scared of.

So Phoebe came to my house. We studied. We talked. We ate popcorn and watched documentaries about the ocean. We laughed. My folks adored her the instant they met her. Life was pretty much perfect.

We started hanging out at my house most days after school. I thought it would become a problem after a while. I figured eventually she'd invite me back to her place. For three weeks, she didn't. But Friday during lunch, she leaned forward over her tray and beckoned me with her finger. I moved closer. She whispered in my ear. The sensation of her warm breath so near my flesh shut down my power of hearing for a moment. But then the words sunk in.

"My parents are going away tonight."

"Oh?" A half-dozen glands shot various overdoses of hormones into my bloodstream.

Phoebe nodded.

"Away?"

"Far away." She smiled. "They won't be home until really late."

Are they taking the cat? "Great."

"We'll have the whole place to ourselves."

Not really. Maybe the cat would stay outside. Panic sent my mind to strange places. I imagined buying a bird and leaving the cage in her front yard. Or dousing myself with some kind of chemical that repelled cats. From there, my mind bombarded me with scenes of Johnny Depp leaping into my lap. I could almost feel his claws digging into my groin.

"You don't seem very interested." Phoebe batted her eyes and made a sound somewhere between a meow and a purr, then said, "Don't tell me you're a scaredy cat."

"Are you kidding? This is fabulous. It's just, my folks want me home for dinner. We're having company."

"No problem. Come over after dinner. It's Friday. We can stay up late." She reached under the table and squeezed my knee, sending a tingle up my thigh that felt nicer than the sting of imaginary cat's claws. "As late as we want."

"It's just a cat. It's just a cat. It's just a cat." No matter how often I said those words, they had no power to change reality. The very word itself— *cat*—could raise my pulse. I could barely eat dinner. When we were done, I kept looking at the clock. It was almost seven. Phoebe was expecting me. And I wanted to go. Man, did I want to go. This was every guy's dream. A hot girl—a girl I really cared about—and an empty house.

But the house wasn't empty. The thought of being a captive plaything of that hideous beast was enough to make me want to slink up to my room, crawl under my covers, and never come out again.

I couldn't go through with it. I'd have to invent some sort of excuse. It was too late to tell her I was allergic to cats. I should have done that the instant he showed up. But I'd been too freaked out to think straight. Maybe I could tell her I'd been grounded. That would work. I wouldn't have to pretend to be disappointed. My disappointment would be real. Very real.

As I reached for the phone, it rang.

"Hello?"

In answer, I heard my name, stretched through several octaves and far more syllables than usual.

"Phoebe?" I asked.

"Uh-huhhh."

"What's wrong?"

"Johnny . . ."

Johnny's dead? I felt a huge wave of guilt over the huge wave of glee that hit me at the thought of Johnny wrapped around the front right tire of a Ford Explorer. But no amount of guilt could drown out the glee.

". . . caught a mouse."

Phoebe hit even higher octaves with the word *mouse,* as if a tiny rodent could be the source of all terror in the world.

"A mouse?"

"Yeah." Three syllables, two octaves.

I waited for more information. Instead of explaining further, Phoebe let out a scream. That was followed by a thump and clatter that did temporary damage to my right ear. I had the feeling she'd dropped the phone.

"Can you hear me?" I shouted.

Distantly, I heard her voice. "Randy, help."

A damsel in distress. The total geekazoid fantasy. If only the cause of the distress had been something I could handle, like a spider or a dragon. Anything except a cat. I didn't want to go. But the fear in her voice lingered in my mind. I knew how she felt. Knew it all too well. She was a prisoner of irrational terror, and she'd reached out to me for help. "Hang on. I'm coming," I shouted into the phone. I headed over to her house.

When I opened the front door, I expected Johnny Depp to leap at my face. There was no sign of him. I forced myself to take a deep breath. "Phoebe?"

"In here."

I followed her voice to the kitchen. She was on a chair. I wasn't super thrilled about the idea of dealing with a dead rodent, but I could handle it. I glanced around the floor, looking for the corpse of Mr. Mouse, hoping he'd died from internal injuries and not loss of blood. The only dead thing I spotted was the handset of the cordless phone. At least there was no sign of the cat. Maybe he'd gone outside to kill again.

"So, where's the mouse?" I asked.

"There." She pointed to an archway that led to the dining room.

The cat walked through the opening and sat on his haunches. The mouse—or at least its lower half—dangled from his mouth, the tail hanging like a limp piece of dirty string.

Before I could move, Johnny Depp opened his mouth and dropped the mouse. It didn't plop on its side or back like a respectable dead rodent. It landed on all fours.

"I think it's still alive," I said.

"Eeeeeeeeee," Phoebe said. Her arms waved like a badly manipulated marionette.

The mouse ran across the kitchen, right toward us. Johnny Depp loped after it, gave it a casual swat, then snatched it up in his jaws again.

"Do something," Phoebe said.

I was already in danger of doing something that would require the services of a very skilled dry cleaner. Johnny sat two feet from us, the mouse dangling from his jaws again.

Eat it. Swallow the damn thing.

Johnny got up and put his front paws on the chair. I knew for sure that if he dropped the mouse near Phoebe's feet, it would lead to her death in some sort of tragic way, and I'd be doomed to spend the rest of my school days alone and then grow into a bitter old man who lived by himself in a small apartment stuffed with piles of yellowing newspapers, ate cold spaghetti right out of the can, and creeped out all the little kids on the block.

He can't bite me if his mouth is full. I looked at Phoebe. I looked at the cat. Oh, crap—it was like being faced with the lady or the tiger. Except I knew what was behind each door.

Phoebe screamed again. Johnny started to open his jaws. Knowing that the next moment would become part of my permanent collection of nightmare memories, I bent down, grabbed the cat around the waist with both hands, and snatched him from the floor. He wriggled but didn't let go of the mouse. I held him at arms' length and raced toward the front door, dropped to my knees, let go with one hand to push open the cat door, then chucked Johnny Depp and the mouse onto the porch.

As the flap fell back in place, I collapsed against the door, blocking the entrance with my back.

I tried to take an inventory of the damage. I hadn't been bitten or scratched, but I was trembling. I still couldn't catch my breath. My heart was hammering like an Uzi set on full automatic. My guts felt like someone had been kneading them to make bread dough. This moment would definitely linger in my mind.

Worse, something else lingered—the memory of a loud scream, all the way from the kitchen to the front door. Not Phoebe's scream. Mine. I'd left a trail marked by my fear. I'd howled like a whipped child, and exposed the bare, naked terror that lived inside of me. I knew that wasn't something that drove the ladies wild. I hoped she'd at least let me leave by the back door so I wouldn't run into the cat.

"Poor Randy."

Soft fingers touched my cheek. Phoebe sat on the floor next to me.

"You were scared?" she asked.

There was no way I could hide the truth. Not when I'd nearly shattered every window in the house with my scream. And no way I could speak yet. My lungs had shriveled to the size of pencil holders. I nodded.

Phoebe reached down and took my hand. "I knew we had a lot in common." She leaned over and gave me a kiss on the cheek. "It's okay to be scared. Mice are so creepy. They completely freak me out. But you got rid of the mouse even though you were afraid of it. That makes you my hero." She punctuated this with another kiss. On the lips.

I still couldn't breathe, but fear didn't get all the blame for that. I returned the kiss. A while later, when I could trust myself to speak, I said, "Maybe we should keep Johnny outside for a bit. There's no such thing as *one* mouse. Who knows what else he might drag in."

"Yeah. Who knows?"

"You don't mind?" I asked.

Phoebe reached behind me and latched the cat door. "Johnny likes it outside."

When I left Phoebe's house late that night, I saw Johnny sitting on the porch, less than five feet from me. The fears came right away, but I thought about how I had carried him out of the kitchen. And survived. That eased the terror just a bit.

I braced myself for him to leap at my face. Instead, he stayed where he was and looked at me with lazy eyes.

"I like her," I said. "I like her a lot."

He turned his head away and licked his flank.

"We're just going to have to get used to each other."

He dropped on his side, arched his back, and stretched out his paws, as if inviting me to scratch him.

"Not quite yet." I walked down the porch and across the lawn. "Maybe never." The thought of petting him made me shiver. But not once, all the way to the street, did I need to look back over my shoulder.

■ ■ ■

ABOUT THE AUTHOR

Anyone who has read David Lubar's novels and short stories—or even his essays—has witnessed his quirky sense of humor, his witty wordplay, and his lively characters. "Claws and Effect" has those same qualities, beginning with the play on words of its title.

About the story, David Lubar says: "I chose cats in an attempt to grow as an artist. My first thought, when presented with phobias as a topic, was to look at my own fears and use one of them (though perhaps transmuted into something less personal and revealing). You can't go wrong looking into your own dark basements for material. But I wanted to try something else, so I decided that it would be an interesting exercise to make the phobic element something I was personally very fond of. I have three cats—named Simon, Layla, and Tybalt. I've had cats as pets for most of my life. So I decided to write about a guy who is terrified of cats. And I'm glad I did."

If you have never read any of David Lubar's other works, you will likely enjoy one or more of his other short stories found in *In the Land of the Lawn Weenies and Other Misadventures; Tripping Over the Lunch Lady; Shattered: Stories of Children and War; Don't Cramp My Style; Destination Unexpected;* and *First Crossing.* If you are ready for a longer work, you'll find *Flip* entertaining, *Wizards of the Game* adventuresome, *Hidden Talents* intriguing, and *Dunk* challenging. Lubar's newest novel, *Sleeping Freshmen Never Lie,* is about a boy who learns, on the day before he starts high school, that his mom is pregnant and he's about to become a big brother for the first time. And stay tuned for a sequel to *Hidden Talents.*

· · ·

Lydia knows how to keep her fear under control.
Until the incident with the . . .

Rutabaga

· · · · ·

Nancy Springer

I never told anybody about the knife thing. Couldn't. I mean, in the world according to my mom, a girl should just deal with whatever, and in school, talking about knives can get a person called into the office. So was I crazy or what, with this weirdness in me?

I guess it was a couple of years before the rutabaga incident. Actually, I didn't tell anybody about it then, either, how freaked I'd been feeling. I just let the clenched fist speak for itself. Or not. My parents still don't have a clue. But at least now I do.

Up till I got to be fourteen, maybe fifteen, I wasn't scared of knives at all. Like, Dad gave each of us kids a pocketknife, because he thought we'd whittle tent pegs or wooden flutes or something, and I used to carry my pearl-handled three-blade knife to school in my book bag before one of my friends told me I could get expelled. Then I, being the oldest, got to pass the heads-up on to my kid brothers. It was no use telling my parents, because they just totally expect us to do things the way they do, no discussion, thank you. My parents are kind of out of touch with the realities of the modern world. They don't watch the news; in fact, we don't have a TV. They married late in life, and they're all about organic gardening and beekeeping and composting and recycling and brown eggs and granola, you know? There's a word for what they are: crunchies.

So I don't remember exactly what year it was, but I totally remember the minute the fear began. There I stood in the kitchen, fixing tomatoes, when Mom poked her nose over my shoulder and said, "For gosh sake, Lydia, you want to make thin, even slices." In her crunchy way, Mom could give Martha Stewart competition. "Don't cut them so thick. That's wasteful." I didn't say anything, because that would have been "talking back." And I didn't think anything, because if I did, then I'd want to say it, so I didn't feel like I was allowed to "think back," either. But while Mom was complaining, something went crooked inside me, something went ugly in my eyes, and just for a blink the tomato was a heart I was hacking into slabs, and the tomato juice was blood all over the butcher block. I mean, I really felt like it was blood, and we don't do blood in my house, ever. It scared me so bad, my hands started shaking.

I made myself finish the tomatoes because I felt like I had to, but my slices were so wobbly, Mom said, "Lydia, what's the matter with you? I know you can handle a knife better than that," and the crooked something in me twisted like an L-wrench, scaring me so bad I knew that I must never touch a sharp knife again, never, or something unthinkably terrible might happen.

Okay, I tried to tell myself, so I was scared; so what? The fear would go away, like the time I'd stayed overnight with my friend Brittany and we saw a huge thousand-legger in the bathtub and Brittany zapped it with hair spray. The bug's feet stuck to the side of the tub as its body broke away and squiggled down the drain, leaving all its legs behind like a pair of false eyelashes glued to the white porcelain, and we both screamed till we could have puked. And then we got into one of our hypothetical debates, this time about whether bugs had a right to live. But in a few days we forgot the whole thing. The weirdness with the knife and the tomato could be like that, something scary to forget about, right?

Wrong.

The fear, like, took up residence in me. Moved in to

stay, always awake and so bad I could just barely hide it, and it never got any better. Every time I walked into the kitchen, I had to turn my eyes away from where Mom kept the sharp knives in a slotted block of wood that stood on the countertop, in plain sight, where anybody could just walk over and grab one by the handle. I could feel the knives there, right out in the open, for gosh sake, like an evil gravitational force straining at my chest and shoulders and the back of my neck. Why couldn't Mom put the knives away in a drawer? She kept the vegetable peelers in a drawer. I'd never used vegetable peelers before I got scared of knives, but I sure did now. They had blunt tips, so I could peel carrots or cucumbers or whatever when Mom told me to. Which was often, because she and Dad were raising us vegetarian. Not vegan, thanks to eggs and cheese, but just the same, we ate vegetables my friends never touched—turnips, eggplant, acorn squash—and some they never heard of: parsnips, salsify, rhubarb, rutabagas.

I never liked rutabagas.

Actually, most of what we ate at home I didn't like, especially beans. Red beans, black beans, kidney beans, pinto beans, baked beans, lima beans, almost every day we had some kind of beans, and I could eat them or go hungry, whichever. Mom and Dad dealt with the fact that I disliked beans the same way they dealt with most things that contradicted them: by ignoring it. Or maybe *ignoring* is not the right word. By not noticing at all. Like, I don't think they were just pretending not to hear me gagging or see the "Yuck" on my face. It was more like they really didn't see anything they didn't want to.

Same with the knife thing. Mom and Dad were oblivious. When I did the dishes, there I'd be with my hands in hot water and the rest of me shivering cold, washing everything except the sharp knives. I'd just leave them in the bottom of the dishpan, and then Mom would get annoyed. She would lecture me about lack of cooperation and sloppy work habits and not finishing my job and no allowance for me that week, but it never dawned on her why I wouldn't touch the knives. Or why, like, if somebody left a knife lying on the countertop, I'd put a dishtowel or a newspaper over it. Or why I'd peel potatoes but I wouldn't cut them up; I'd just throw them in the pot whole, then get another lecture about being lazy and you're grounded, young lady.

This went on, like I said, for a couple of years. In the kitchen was the worst. Every minute I spent there, my teeth clenched, my heart pounded, I sweated hot and cold, my neck and jaws ached, and something roared and surged like Niagara Falls inside my head. In the dining room wasn't so bad, although even butter knives scared me some. In the bathroom, I had to keep my eyes away from Dad's razor and Mom's nail file. In my bedroom, the pocketknife Dad had given me lurked in my dresser drawer, where I couldn't see it, but I could still feel it in there like a dark, wicked kind of magnetic force.

Sometimes I couldn't sleep.

Because of the dream. Same one, over and over. Me and my whole family at the lake on a sunny day, white sand beach, water slide, everybody swimming and having a good time, even Mom splashing and smiling, but then the surface of the water would erupt with hard points and Dad would yell, "Sharks!" But the points weren't shark fins; they were the sharp tips of huge knives rising out of the lake in a forest of blades, and the lake wasn't a lake anymore, it was a God-size dishpan and we were, like, the dirty stuff getting washed, and the knives . . .

I always jolted awake, sitting up in bed biting my lip, before the knives did anything. Just knowing they were there under the water was bad enough.

Summertime was the worst—all those vegetables to freeze or can. Someday, I swore to myself, I'd eat only vegetables that came from the supermarket already cut up in little bags. Meanwhile, while Mom was working her crunchy part-time job at the Earth Shoe outlet, I was supposed to take care of stuff at home. I'd dig potatoes, turnips, carrots, beets, whatever. I'd pick peas and pod them, pick green beans and wash them and snap them. I'd pick corn and husk it and cook it, but I wouldn't cut the kernels off the cobs.

"What is the matter with you?" Mom blew up one

day when she came home to stacks of corn in the kitchen. "Lydia, I swear, you are the laziest, most ungrateful, most contrary daughter on the face of this poor neglected planet."

And I felt that awful stab of blood-colored tomato-red fear again.

September saved me. Thank school. The only place I felt safe and okay was in school, where even the scissors had blunt tips. There, I could relax, because no sharp objects of any kind were allowed. The administrators and teachers were all paranoid about pocketknives, craft knives, box cutters, nail clippers, anything like that. They knew, like I knew, that those were dangerous, evil things that could hurt somebody.

"I can't believe," Brittany said to me across the cafeteria table at lunchtime, "they won't let me make a woodprint in the art room."

This was junior year, and Brittany was trying to put together an art portfolio for college interviews. She'd been talking about a really good idea for some prints.

"Or even a linoleum block print. They say they got rid of the press and the rollers and everything."

"Huh?" I wasn't paying much attention because I was distracted by what she was eating, which was a roast beef sandwich. I mean, pink, with like, blood seeping out. I knew that was normal for most people, yet I didn't see how anybody could cut into something bloody and call it food. Just the thought of blood . . .

Tomato.

Sharp knife. Mom nagging at me.

I felt cold.

"They say because of budget," Brittany was complaining, "but that's bullshit. You know it's because they're scared to let kids use the tools. What do they think, I'm going to take a gouge or a knife and stick it into a teacher?"

The word *knife* always bothered me, and right at that particular moment it jolted me so bad I went, "Uh."

"What's the matter, Liddy?"

Because it was okay to argue with Brittany, I actually kind of said what I was thinking. "Um, what if you did?"

"Huh?"

"I mean, it happens. What if you, um, stuck the knife in the teacher?"

"Oh, thanks a lot."

"No, I mean hypothetically, what if you wanted to?"

"I wouldn't, that's all. Duh."

"But if you got, like, mad, and you had a knife in your hand . . ."

"That's stupid. A knife's not going to make me do anything I decide not to."

"But what if you got really pissed off?"

"Then I'd say I was pissed. Or yell, or throw something, or stomp out, or better yet, draw a pissed-off picture. What if you got really pissed off?"

"I, um, I don't know."

Brittany put down her roast beef sandwich and stared at me.

"Liddy," she said, "you've got to stop keeping the lid on so much."

I thought it was one of her lame jokes. I had no idea what she was talking about.

Until I got home.

Not that day. It might have been a week or two afterward. I got home from school and there was Mom in my face before I even put my books down. "Liddy, let me show you how to fix this rutabaga for supper."

Most nights I made supper because she had to go to work. And it wasn't okay to just, like, throw a cheese pizza in the oven, either. I had to make supper the way Mom would have done it.

So there on the kitchen counter sat the biggest, ugliest rutabaga I'd ever seen. The size it was, and the blobby shape, and the muddy color—if it had been hanging from a tree, anybody would have thought it was a hornet's nest. But it would never hang from a tree, because it weighed as much as a bowling ball. It was plenty big enough to feed all of us, if anybody could stand to eat it at all.

"Mom," I pointed out, careful not to sound like I was complaining, "that thing will be as tough as polystyrene."

"So whose fault is it that it got left in the ground too long?" Mine, she meant. Everything was always my fault.

"Rather than let it go to waste," she lectured more quietly, "what you do is, dice it very small and . . ."

And I had no idea what she said after that, because my mind stuck like old gray chewing gum on "dice it very small."

Mom wanted me to reduce the monster rutabaga to little bitty cubes.

Cut it up.

With a knife.

I couldn't do it.

But I had to, or Mom would know there was something wrong with me.

All the Lydia in me kind of fled my body and hovered in the corner, watching, while the physical me stood there like a potato on a nail.

"You have to get it started now, Liddy," Mom was saying sharply. "Get moving."

So I moved.

I walked to the woodblock that held the knives. For the first time in a couple of years I grabbed one by the handle. I pulled it out. The steel blade glinted all shivery like water when the wind blows, because my hand was quivering.

I turned around. Mom was standing right there.

I lifted the knife and said, "I love you, Mom."

Mom gave a puzzled frown, because I'd hardly ever said this before except on special occasions.

But it was true. I stabbed the razor-sharp point of the knife into the rutabaga.

"Um, I love you, too, um, sweetie." Mom sounded uncertain of her script. "That's why I, um, try to teach you how to do things right. I'll be back to show you what else is for supper." She buzzed off to get dressed for her job.

I yanked the knife out of the rutabaga and stood there, not shaking anymore, hefting it by the handle and feeling the weight and balance of the blade, and also feeling all the Lydia run back into me and grin.

Not afraid.

I knew I wouldn't have that stupid nightmare anymore, either.

Brittany was right. A knife couldn't make me do anything I decided not to.

And as a corollary, neither could Mom.

That rutabaga was so big and so tough, trying to cut it was like tackling a coconut with a machete. But I felt like a superhero, so strong, so sure, and I knew exactly what I wanted to do. What I had decided to do.

Sitting the rutabaga on its cut stem end like a head on a neck, I whacked away its thick brown ridgy scalp, leaving fibrous flesh the color of raw chicken skin. Then I started to carve, like a sculptor carving wood, which was what that rutabaga was about as hard as.

Or more like a guy roughing a statue out of a tree

trunk with a chain saw, actually. It helped that the rutabaga was kind of the right shape to start with. From time to time I consulted my own hand for reference. Once I'd gotten the basic cuts in place, all I had to do was shape a thumb as best I could, then put grooves between the closed fingers. When I heard Mom coming downstairs, I set my masterpiece in the middle of the dining-room table and yelled, "Dinner, everybody."

Like seventeen-year locusts, my dad and brothers appeared out of nowhere, noisy and eager to feed. They quieted down quickly, though, when all they saw was a rutabaga hacked into the shape of an upright, clenched fist.

"You can eat it raw," I told them.

Behind me I heard a scream. That would be Mom.

"Lydia," she demanded, "what is the meaning of this?"

I turned and faced her quietly enough. "You tell me."

"What I told you was to cube it, braise it, and simmer it in apple juice for two hours!"

"I'm not keeping the lid on anymore," I said.

"Lydia!" Dad barked. "Don't talk back."

"Which leaves me with what options?"

Both of my parents, not to mention my brothers, stood staring at me totally bewildered. Mom started blinking hard as she said, "Young lady, go to your room. Just go to your room and stay there until I say you can come out." Blink, blink. "The way you've been acting lately—I don't know." Blink, blink, blink. "You used to be such a good girl. I just don't understand what's happened to you." Blink. *"Go."*

I have to admit that after I'd slammed my bedroom door—and we never slam doors in my house—after I had flung myself onto my bed, I cried a little, but mostly from relief. It didn't matter whether Mom understood—I knew she probably never would—because now I did. I understood me. And the next time I had that blood-red feeling, I'd face the simple fact that I was pissed off, and I'd speak it and I'd show it, instead of going around like a dummy thinking I had to be afraid of knives.

Sitting up on my bed, I wiped my eyes with a tissue, blew my nose, wadded the Kleenex, and tossed it in the trash. Then I smiled as I reached over to pull open a dresser drawer.

It felt awesome to open my pearl-handled pocketknife again without fear. Just caution, which is a very different feeling, a good feeling, being careful not to hurt myself. After I thumbed the blades to select the sharpest one, I began to carve an *L* on the wooden headboard of my bed. Mom was going to be totally torqued when she saw it, but too bad; who slept here, anyway? Me. Not just initials, I decided, cutting the strong straight lines. My whole name. Not *Liddy*, either. *LYDIA.*

■ ■ ■

ABOUT THE AUTHOR

"I chose to write about a phobia of knives," Nancy Springer confesses, "because I've suffered through the experience myself, for the same reason—repressed anger. So I could write with authority about Lydia's problem. Woodcarving helped me, although I show no talent whatsoever and consider that I'd better stick to writing for my main creative outlet."

Writing has obviously been an extremely good outlet for her creativity. This resident of East Berlin, Pennsylvania, has published short stories, poetry, books for children and teenagers, and novels for adults. Some young readers know her best for her novels about horses, such as *Colt, A Horse to Love, Not on a White Horse, The Boy on a Black Horse,* and *The Hex Witch of Seldom.* Others know her best for her fantasy adventure novels, such as her modern interpretations of the King Arthur legends from Camelot—*I Am Mordred* and *I Am Morgan le Fay*—and her Rowan Hood tales set in the world of Robin Hood: *Rowan Hood: Outlaw Girl of Sherwood Forest, Lionclaw, Outlaw Princess of Sherwood,* and *Wild Boy.* The next and final volume in that series will be *Rowan Hood Returns.* Most of her protagonists are misfits and outcasts, as they are in both of her Edgar Allan Poe Award–winning young adult mysteries: *Toughing It* and *Looking for Jamie Bridger.* In addition to winning those coveted Edgar Awards, she has also been a finalist for the Hugo Award, the World Fantasy Award, and the Nebula Award.

In her spare time, Nancy Springer likes to fish—"from a

rowboat," she says. "No motorboat for me. No fancy fishing gear, either; just the basic hook, line, and sinker."

And by the way, she says, "as research for my story, I bought a huge rutabaga and hacked at it. I am definitely over my own phobia of knives."

. . .

Only one thing stands in Josh's way of becoming a senior.
But time is running out before . . .

Bang, Bang, You're Dead

. . . . .

Jane Yolen and Heidi E. Y. Stemple

Bang, bang, you're dead!
  It's a game little kids play. But some kids don't play it—they live it.
  On the night of July 31, 1957, Michael Farmer, a 15-year-old boy partially crippled by polio, was beaten and stabbed to death in a New York City park near his home.

Declamations, in Hatfield, Massachusetts, is a big, fancy word for you-all-have-to-give-a-speech-and-that-means-everyone. The dictionary would define it as a speech or presentation spoken in a formal and theatrical style. I would define it as hell. It's my high school's way of making up for the fact that we are the smallest public high school in Massachusetts. *Overcompensating,* which means going overboard, trying too hard.

Every junior has to write, memorize, and present a declamation in English class. No excuse will get you out of doing one. And trust me—every excuse has been tried: grandparents' deaths, full-blown asthma attacks, a bomb scare at the school. Last year one girl got pregnant, but she was a month away from giving birth and she still had to give her declamation. It was about diapers. And hilariously funny.

The top four boys and the top four girls in the class, as chosen by the English teachers, have to give the speech again a week later on Declamation Night in front of the whole town. Everyone shows up—parents, siblings, teachers, the town cops, the selectmen and selectwomen, classmates, even last year's graduates, at least the ones who didn't move very far away. It's a circus.

And the winners—one boy, one girl—then have to memorize the Gettysburg Address and the first two long paragraphs of the Declaration of Independence, which they get to perform at graduation.

When my older brother Aaron, the family's golden

boy, won the top prize—if having to memorize Lincoln's words can be said to be a prize—no one was surprised. He did it in typical Aaron fashion, refusing to stand at the podium. He stood in front of it. And when he was done, it took a full minute for the audience to catch its collective breath and start clapping. He had stunned them. He was that good. He was always that good.

Aaron was obsessed with street gangs. Ever since he read *The Outsiders* in seventh grade, he'd wanted alternately to be in a street gang and to help kids who were in them. No one, not Aaron or anyone else, ever seriously believed he would wind up in one. Aaron was too perfect to slip into the dark side of things.

Bang, bang, you're dead!

His first line got the audience's attention. Then he told the story of a real kid who was killed in 1950s gang fighting. A real sad story. I swear, half the audience was tearing up. He was completely at ease up there. He didn't even bring the one index card you're allowed. Just spoke.

Aaron and I couldn't have been less like brothers if we tried. He was born blond and tall and perfect. The star of the basketball team and the debate team. Straight A's and colleges offering him full scholarships. That doesn't happen every day in a town as ignored by outsiders as our town is.

Now, where Aaron's tall, I'm short. Where he's broad, I'm scrawny. I'm not smart, am hardly athletic, and not one girl has ever tried to go out with me. I used to be blond. We did have that in common, but I dyed my hair black last November. I thought it made me look vaguely cool. My mother said it just made me look silly. Dad called it stupid. Aaron just smiled when he saw it.

"Goth," he said.

"Not," I said. "No eyeliner. No vampires. No cloaks." But secretly I was pleased. If Aaron thought I was a Goth, so would others. And then they would know I was not trying to be him. I mean, even if I wanted to, how could I compete?

Me, I'm a reader. I hide behind books. I know words, by definition, but not to say them aloud. Not to crowds anyway.

Aaron, he could walk into a crowd of people and own it just by talking. I see any kind of crowd and if I can't disappear, then the whole room starts to sway and roll like the ocean. My head roars and my vision closes down, into a white light. My throat tightens and I start shaking. I have always avoided crowds at all costs. And speaking in front of them only doubles the panic attack.

I have glossophobia. That is, fear of speaking, or of trying to speak, in public. So is it any wonder that the idea of having to give a declamation was my idea of hell?

While I was worrying about one measly speech—*measly* meaning tiny, insignificant, small—Aaron was finishing college. Harvard and Yale had wanted him, but he had decided on Columbia, right in the heart of street-gang territory. He was graduating an entire year early, of course. That was Aaron—rushing headlong into life, taking summer school courses and extra credits. Never counting the cost. Maybe he thought he was immortal. I sure did.

I know he thought about going on to law school eventually, and he'd already been offered jobs at lots of firms—in all kinds of fields—but first he was finishing up an internship program with Brotherhood Now, an offshoot of the New York City police department, working with street gangs. Whenever I spoke to him on the phone, he always started out by saying, "And you think those Springfield kids are tough . . ." though in fact I'd never met any Springfield kids. I mean, Hatfield is small, rural, and a half-hour north of Springfield, western Massachusetts' idea of big urban sprawl. Then Aaron would tell me all about the latest gang incidents. Of course he never told Mom and Dad those stories. They'd have freaked out and insisted he come home.

Come home! As if what they wanted could have changed his mind. He'd have just given them his glorious smile, waved his grades at them, and done any damned thing he wanted to.

The last time he called, he asked me how the declamations were going. Of course he remembered it was that time of year.

"Picked your topic yet?" he said, though the way he

phrased it made me realize he knew that once again I was going to mess up.

It was three weeks before declamations and I hadn't turned in the rough draft yet. Rough draft? Hah! I hadn't even turned in the outline. I kept thinking: *It's better to get incompletes than F's. Better to get F's than stand up and speak before a crowd.* But you can't pass English and become a senior if you don't do your declamation, so I think Mr. Ashe, my English teacher, was being lenient—trying to help me. Or rather, to help himself. I don't think any of my teachers, especially Mr. Ashe, wanted to have to suffer through another junior year with me. Or else he was remembering my golden brother and giving me the benefit of the doubt.

It wasn't like I wasn't trying. I told Aaron that.

"Honest, I sit down at my desk, shut the windows and door, and crank the music up high, as if that can chase away the fear."

He laughed at me, not a mean laugh, but one of those "Oh, brother!" laughs.

"Nothing to be afraid of, Josh," he said. "Picture them all in their underwear."

"Yeah, sure," I said. "Adrienna Snyder in her underwear will do wonders for my confidence." I can always be funny around Aaron. Not because I'm funny, but because he puts everyone at ease.

"Then picture the English teachers in their underwear."

"Do English teachers wear underwear?" I asked. And

we both had a good laugh. And then he told me the latest about the gangs he was working with, the Lords and the Sharks.

"Is it going well?" I asked. Not because I wanted to know but because I thought someone in the family should know.

"Better than expected," he said. "I think they trust me."

"Of course they trust you," I said. "You are a declamation winner. 'Bang, bang, you're dead! It's a game little kids play. But some kids don't play it—they live it.'"

"That's good," he said. "Maybe you could just recycle my speech."

"Yeah, like no one will remember it's yours."

"Don't worry," he said. "You'll rise to the occasion."

I snorted. "And then fall on my face."

"Give Mom and Dad my love," he said, and hung up.

I went back to the desk and thought about my declamation, just trying to get an idea. But the minute I started thinking about it, everything closed in on me. My vision. My throat. My skin. The walls. If I'd been wearing a shirt with a collar, it would have strangled me.

I stood up and opened the window and drew in a great big gulp of air, thinking that if I didn't, I might pass out or throw up. But it was no use. Just thinking about the declamation and the crowd I'd have to face gave me the shakes. So I did the only thing I could do. I stopped trying.

* * *

A week went by, two. Mr. Ashe stopped asking me about my project or the notes or the outline of my declamation. Instead he sent me to the principal's office, where I spent every English class lying on a couch and reading *The Lord of the Rings* for the ninth time.

Aaron called every evening and tried to help. He offered to come home and work with me.

"The gangs trust you," I said. "They need you. The Lords. The Sharks."

"Actually," he said, "I'm not working with the Sharks anymore. The Sharks swim in deeper waters now."

"What does that mean?"

He laughed. Then he changed the subject. "What's your topic?"

I laughed back. Said nothing. Nothing about the declamations, the principal's office, the couch, *The Lord of the Rings*. Nothing.

"That bad, eh?"

"Oh, nothing is ever that bad," I said. But it was, though I told him nothing.

The next time Aaron called, I let Mom talk to him. No use having everyone mad at me.

And then it was the day before the declamations. At home I was still trying to come up with something, though at school I maintained a kind of joking nonchalance.

Nonchalance—that means I was acting as if nothing bothered me.

But everything bothered me, and every time I tried to put my hands on the keyboard to write something, no matter how lame, I began to sweat and cough. I tried thinking of people—the teachers, the judges, the other students, Angelina Jolie, anyone—in their underwear, just as Aaron had suggested. All those semi-naked people staring at me as I . . . gave a speech.

It made things worse.

So that's when I decided to quit school. To run away. Nothing extreme. Just the Antarctic. Or the North Pole. Or the Galápagos Islands. Places without declamations or explanations or any -ations at all.

I had actually gotten to the point of contemplating what to bring with me—my iPod, an extra pair of Vans, three black T-shirts—when the phone rang. I figured it was Aaron checking up on me again, because he knew that the next day was The Day.

So I eased the phone from the cradle after someone else picked it up downstairs. I pressed the TALK button as gently and—I hoped—as silently as was possible. And I sat down to listen in.

It wasn't Aaron.

But it was about Aaron.

"Mrs. Kendall?" came a deep voice.

"Yes?" That was Mom. "Speaking."

"Ma'am, this is Johnson Atticus. I am the director of Brotherhood Now. I am afraid I have some dire news."

Dire. I thought. *Rhymes with fire. And expire.* Not comforting.

Just then the doorbell rang as well. I took the phone with me. I had to. It was all but stuck to my ear. I looked over the stair rail to our front door, which Dad was just opening. Officer Weeks, round-shouldered and familiar, was standing there, his cap in hand.

"Tom," he said, "better sit down." He grabbed Dad by the elbow and moved him into the living room.

And that was when I knew for sure. It didn't take a genius.

Aaron was dead.

The phone slipped from my hand and crashed to the floor. But Mom never heard it. There was nothing left to hear.

I was wrong, of course: there *was* an excuse that worked for getting me out of declamations. No one expected me to go to school, much less participate.

A week later, at Aaron's funeral, dozens of people got up to say something about him. They couldn't help themselves. His coaches—in sports and debate. Teachers and students. The chief of police. The selectmen and select-women. People had even driven up from New York to talk about the work Aaron had been doing. His college friends showed up in SUVs and vans loaded with coeds. My entire junior class, most of whom avoided me every other day, took up the entire back of the room, silent witnesses.

Everyone hugged me. There wasn't a moment I thought I could breathe without counting each breath. "In and out, in and out, in and out," I chanted to myself. If I stopped counting, I thought, I might forget how to breathe and simply turn blue. But who cared? I certainly didn't.

I actually tried to stand when the priest asked if anyone else had anything they wanted to say. I wanted to tell them that Aaron had been a great big brother and that I would miss him. That he had walked me to school on my first day of kindergarten because Mom had had a migraine that sidelined her. That when I had pneumonia and was in the hospital, he'd begged to be allowed to sleep in a cot by my side—and did. That he was the one who taught me to ride a bike, to ski, to skateboard, and to play chess. He had given me my first Tolkien book.

But every time I tried to stand, my head started swimming and my knees buckled. And in that moment of hesitation, another friend or teacher stood first and *testified*—that means spoke out loud in a truthful manner—about Aaron's awesome achievements. So I ended up saying nothing.

I thought I could hear his voice in my ear: "When it's your time, you'll rise to the occasion." But if your brother's funeral isn't the time, then when is?

I got through it. My mother didn't. Luckily her doctor was at the funeral and when she fainted, he helped her get back home. Dad was useless, sitting and drinking, though he'd been in AA for years. People came and went: Aaron's friends and Aaron's teachers and Aaron's boss and Aaron's old girlfriends. When almost everyone had gone except my grandparents, a couple of aunts, and Mom's three best friends, I slipped out.

No one noticed.

I didn't know where I was walking. Or for how long. At some point I started going faster and faster and faster until finally I was running.

It was dusk. Not quite dark and not quite light. The air was moist, muggy, maybe even raining a bit, but I didn't notice. My feet hitting the pavement made my brain rattle in my skull. Water ran down my face. Rain. Sweat. Tears.

Suddenly I stopped and doubled over, hands on knees. I gasped, heaving as if hit by a tsunami. *Tsunami*—a giant wave. My legs felt like cooked spaghetti noodles. My brain felt swollen. Lots of metaphors, all mixed. I wiped furiously at my eyes, blurring them with dirty hands.

I looked up, saw where I was. Knew where I was. I was at the only place I could make things right. I was where I could make Aaron proud of me. Become who only he knew I could be. I opened the door to my school and walked in.

The gym was full. Full of people. A crowd, a mob, an audience. Of course! It was Declamation Night.

I didn't stop. I walked down the aisle of chairs, through the people listening intently to Anabelle Kennedy, who was doing her declamation at the podium.

I couldn't hear what she was saying. The world roared in my ears. My vision closed down like an old-fashioned TV set turning off until all I could see was a pinpoint of light directly in front of me. I kept walking toward that spot. My throat had swelled almost shut. And this was the most normal I had felt in a week. At least this horrible feeling was one I recognized.

I kept walking.

Down the aisle.

Up the stairs.

Onto the stage.

Up to the podium.

At some point, everyone must have noticed me. Anabelle stopped talking, her mouth still open, shaped like an O. I faced the students in their chairs behind her.

Reaching out, my hands gripped the podium, which suddenly felt like a rock, still and solid. Then I turned to face the town.

I saw Mr. Ashe stand and take a step toward the stage. Ms. Johansen, the principal, reached out and held his arm to stop him.

Grabbing the mike, I started speaking. The words came rolling out.

> *Bang, bang, you're dead!*
> *It's a game little kids play.*
> *But some kids don't play it—they live it.*
> *On the night of May 17, 2004, my brother,*
> *Aaron Kendall, was shot to death in a New York*
> *City park near where he worked with the very kids*
> *who killed him. They were just little fish in the great*
> *sea of the city, but he was a fisherman who'd been*
> *trying to save them. And they reeled him in. . . .*

When I finished, there was a hush, a silence so huge I thought I would throw up into it. And then the audience stood and applauded, so loudly I know I'd have collapsed if Anabelle hadn't held me up.

I won the declamations—but I didn't—because I hadn't actually been one of the finalists. So I was not allowed to give the Gettysburg Address in front of the crowd at graduation. Thank goodness for that.

But I memorized the speech anyway.

I didn't have a large audience when I delivered it, the dirt still fresh on Aaron's grave. On my knees, speaking to the gravestone, I began: "Four score and seven years ago . . ." Not a large audience, but a tough one. I got through it without a bobble and felt sure that I could see Aaron. He was grinning broadly.

■ ■ ■

ABOUT THE AUTHORS

Heidi E. Y. Stemple comes from a family of authors—father David Stemple, brothers Adam and Jason, and mother Jane Yolen. Jane, of course, is one of the most productive and versatile authors in the world, having published more than 250 books, including children's picture books, novels for middle-grade readers, young adult novels, nonfiction, short stories, books for adults, and even a comic book. She has written historical fiction, biographies, mysteries, adventures, songbooks, essays, and poems; has retold fairy tales and folktales; re-imagined fantastical creatures such as unicorns, werewolves, and dragons; and has compiled and edited anthologies of short stories. Among the awards she and her books have earned are two Christopher Medals, two Nebula Awards, a Caldecott Medal, a World Fantasy Award, a Golden Kite Award, a Lewis Carroll Shelf Award, several Best Book of the Year awards, a California Young Reader Medal, and the Kerlan Award.

Compared to her mother, Heidi Stemple has been writing

for a relatively brief time. She first worked with emotionally disturbed and incarcerated children, then was a probation/parole officer, a private investigator, a waitress, and a stay-at-home mom with two daughters. In addition to publishing poems and short stories on her own, Heidi has collaborated with her mother on a number of projects before writing "Bang, Bang, You're Dead." They are coauthors of the Unsolved Mysteries from History series, which includes *The Mary Celeste, The Wolf Girls, Roanoke: The Lost Colony,* and *The Salem Witch Trials;* as well as *Mirror, Mirror,* a collection of folktales and fairy tales from around the world with a mother-and-daughter theme; and *The Barefoot Book of Ballet Stories.* Their most interesting collaboration has been *Dear Mother, Dear Daughter: Poems for Young People,* in which poems in the voice of an adolescent girl (written by Heidi) addressing events and issues in her life (such as homework, phone calls, ear piercing, self-image, allowances, and romance) are printed on the left-hand page, and poem-responses in the voice of the girl's mother (written by Jane) appear on the right-hand page. A perfect book for pre-teenage girls to read with their mothers.

As for how they came to write "Bang, Bang" together, Jane says: "Most of the time, I have an idea for a story—a character, a setting, a first line—and then just sit down and let it develop." But Jane and Heidi were driving to a conference to give a speech together, and Heidi suggested it. She says, "I threw it out there because, unlike my mother, even though I speak professionally, I have a pretty bad fear of speaking in public. In fact, after six years of doing it, I still feel dizzy and nauseous before almost every speech. Aaron's declamation opening in the story is my real speech from High School Declamations—that much is true. Even though I had threatened to quit school if I had to give the speech, I managed to get through it, not once, but twice, and came in first runner-up."

Jane recalls: "We had a long drive, and by the time we were a half hour into it, we knew the entire plot of the story—just worked the whole thing out and then promptly forgot it for several months. Luckily, Heidi still has her memory cells."

"I actually not only have no fear of public speaking," proclaims Jane. "I love it. I am a ham. I even do professional storytelling. I have a hard time wondering what all the fuss is about, but none of my three children (all book-making adults) actually enjoys public speaking."

. . .

Will's life would be easier if his surroundings were a . . .

No Clown Zone

. . . . .

Gail Giles

It was taped to my locker Monday morning.

A clown. Stuffed-doll variety. A big X of duct tape holding it fast. From a slit in the front of the clown's polka-dot pants hung a noodle. Cooked and limp variety. A bright sign with big, easy-to-read letters dangled from the clown's shiny red nose: *PLOP goes the Weasel.* Clutched in the clown's hand was a big pill. Blue variety. Little tag on it: *Get the pill, Wilting Will.*

Why won't asteroids hit the earth on cue?

I stood there, and the questions and comments bounced off my ears without wiggling in. All I could see was that clown. That evil, smiling, red-nosed clown. I wanted to rip it off my locker and stomp it to tatters, but I couldn't make myself touch it. I tried to back away, but the lookey loos were behind me and having too much fun. Clown fear almost lost the battle with full-on embarrassment. Make that old-fashioned shame. My manhood was now an object of ridicule in front of everyone who mattered.

My life officially sucked. Because of clowns.

"Dude, Third Date Lisa takes it hard when somebody refuses the offer, now doesn't she? The girl just don't take no with a smile."

Houston, whose mother's most outstanding quirk was to name her children for the town of their conception (brother Cheyenne, sister Boston), reached out and jerked the clown free. "Will, I don't think this Bozo looks like you at all." He held it up high, turning it for the audience to view. "His nose is too little and his pecker . . . well, I've never eyeballed your pecker, so I couldn't say." He flicked off the offensive noodle. "And from what you told me, Third Date Lisa didn't see it, either."

Houston tossed the clown up and out. Somebody snagged it. Houston turned back to me and mock-punched my shoulder. "This is your own fault, Bad Boy. You play hard to get, you piss the ladies off. It's just wrong."

I was saved by the bell. Literally. The warning bell rang. The big clot of people broke into small clots and spun off in different directions. Houston grabbed my elbow and steered me away. "What in the shit happened? Cancel that. I got the main idea. I want facts, not the excuse. The clown thing."

My mouth flopped open like a guppy.

"Don't even," Houston said. "The clown thing is *over.* Right now. *Over.* Get used to it. Clown fear is almost funny, but not when it screws up what's really important."

What's really important.

Getting laid.

I don't know why I'm afraid of clowns. I know it doesn't make sense. And I don't know how it started either. A serial killer clown didn't massacre Great Aunt Bertha. I never watched a movie about an evil clown. No birthday party clown got up into my grille and breathed whiskey fumes up my little boy nostrils. But I see a white face and painted-on smile and get the shaking jeebies and want to heave my hamburger.

My mother thinks I'm amusing. My father thinks I'm a wuss. My friends think it's freaky, but don't seem to mind. It appears that's changed. The minding part. The freak part seems to have amped up.

Houston has been my best friend since we were zygotes. He is the school football star and sex god. And aside from being a slut, he is a decent guy. His sister, Boston, is a senior, the no-contest front-runner for valedictorian, and a very "out" lesbian. She's president of the Gay-Straight Alliance. Houston is the most visible part of the straight alliance part. I'm a part too, but my presence doesn't give it the same cred that Houston's does.

Houston, Slacker, another of our friends, and Boston were nose-to-nose in conversation when I shuffled up to our lunch table at noon. They stopped talking the minute I stepped within earshot.

"Now, talk about wrong," I said. "That's wrong."

"We're having a privileged conversation with our attorney," Houston said, pointing to his sister.

"Congratulations on passing the bar, Boston."

"Thanks, I passed three last night. Can't get in until you're twenty-one, don'tcha know."

"Cute," I said. I sat next to Houston. "What are you plotting?"

"Be home tonight and you'll find out," Boston said. "Right now, Calculus is calling me. And it has *such* a sexy voice." She stood, then flicked her brother's ear with her index finger. "Play nice with your teachers."

"Like that's fun," Houston complained. Boston had the rep for smart; Houston's rep was for smart-assed.

"Hi, Will."

Third Date Lisa stood in front of me with a herd of her pouty-lipped friends. She held her index finger straight up then curled it down—wilting. "Seen any clowns lately?" Her friends mimicked the finger-wilt.

"Lisa, honey," Houston drawled. "Homecoming is just around the corner."

Fingers vanished.

Houston grinned. "I wouldn't think that any first stringers would ask a girl to Homecoming if she was putting the hurt on a team member."

Third Date Lisa flushed. The girls closest to her stepped away to put a little geography between them.

Houston, knowing how to work a gap, edged next to Carrie Lewis and slid one arm around her shoulders. "Walk me to class, darlin'. Sometimes I get awful confused in these halls."

Carrie lit up, turned with Houston to leave, then shot Lisa a death stare over her shoulder.

Houston paused, then rocked back on his heel and looked over his shoulder at me. "See you later, Will."

"Yeah, Will, bye," Carrie said.

The rest of the herd chorused the goodbyes.

Third Date Lisa tapped a foot and caved. "Bye, Will. See you later, maybe?"

I was plugged into my iPod and deep into misery music when the twins and Slacker breezed into my room. Houston and Boston are twins. Their mother isn't sure on which end of a vacation they were conceived.

Slacker reached out, tugged the buds from my ears, the iPod from my fingers, turned it off, rolled the wires, and tucked the whole thing into my nightstand drawer. His nickname is ironic. His dad says Slacker was born the hour he was expected, with a day planner clutched in his hand. He's not obsessive compulsive, but he is obsessive. He's also the wide receiver to Houston's quarterback. He's long, lean, and fast, and Houston doesn't even have to look before he unleashes his tight bullet-passes. Slacker's always there, hands ready. He never misses an appointment.

I'm the third leg of the triangle. I'm the refrigerator-shaped guy who puts his shoulder into anybody coming toward the quarterback while he's in the pocket. I guard Houston so he can pass to Slacker.

Slacker was sorting through my clothes. "This goes." He waved a baseball cap that sported CLOWNS in the middle of a circle crossed with a diagonal slash. He put it down. "This, too." Slacker held a T-shirt with the slogan CAN'T SLEEP. CLOWNS WILL EAT ME. I had a couple of those in different colors. Along with Ts and sweatshirts that read I HATE CLOWNS. NO CLOWN ZONE. CLOWNS SUCK. CLOWNS ARE HUMOR CHALLENGED. If it was manufactured, someone had thought it was a clever gift. All the paraphernalia had words, no images.

"Don't you ever hang anything? How many of these do you have?" Slacker piled my anti-clown stuff.

"Scootch over." Boston's hip bumped my shoulders and she leaned against the headboard. She flipped a notebook open. "'*Coulrophobia,*'" she said. "'Persistent, abnormal, and irrational fear of clowns.' That would be you. 'Symptoms include shortness of breath . . .'" She looked, I nodded, she checked her list. "'Irregular heartbeat'?" Glance, nod, check. "'Sweating'?" Check. "'Nausea'?" Check plus. "'Overall feeling of dread.'" She didn't wait for my nod. "Check."

Slacker hauled a duffel out of my closet. He folded each T-shirt and packed it with precision. Houston paced the floor, slamming my football from one hand to another.

"Read him that stuff about lost opportunities, Boss."

I sat up and made the referee's time-out signal. "Hey. Hello. Time. I'm *in* the room."

They looked at me like I had just come out of a coma.

"And?" Houston said.

"And I'd like to know what's going on here. Slacker is packing my clothes, you're wearing out my carpet, and Boston is, I don't know, doing a research paper?"

"This is an intervention," Houston said. "We're telling you that you have a problem. We're going to make you face it and then we're gonna fix you right up."

I couldn't say anything at first. Then Slacker refolded a shirt already folded to mechanical precision.

"You're Harpo, Chico, and Groucho—how can you stage an intervention? You're part of the freak team."

"Excuse me," Boston said. "Those two are certainly

freaks, but are you calling my sexual orientation or my large frontal lobe freakish?" She tapped her forehead.

"Gotcha—sorry, Boss. Your smart part makes you freaky. I'm not used to being around functioning brains. Look at them."

"Hey, even Slacker's been laid," Houston said. "That makes you the interventee and us the interventers."

"May 7, 12:52 A.M., 1487 Collins Avenue, den couch. Parents overnighting in New Orleans," Slacker said. "Donna Lowe. Both of us were scared shitless." He zipped the duffel shut, gazed at the ceiling, and smiled. "It rocked."

"I'm such a loser," I said.

"This isn't the first time the clown thing kept you from scoring," Houston said. "You don't get over this— you'll die a virgin." He drilled the football into my chest.

Houston was right. I date, but girls see me as one of those big, teddy bear guys. The safe date. Slacker goes for girls who like the brainy kind, but the brainy girls find me—um, they pretty much don't want to find me at all. I get the girls who date me to get close to Houston. The girls who want the bad boy, the dangerous guy, and I'm the safe placeholder.

I chest-thump with the guys, but I don't know shit about how to make moves on girls. I know what I want to do, but I don't know how to make that first motion, how to put myself out there. So my experience hasn't gone much past a good-night kiss, though I've lied about a lot more.

Houston referred to a night we doubled to a party, then went to Houston's parents' beach house. Houston and his date disappeared to one bedroom, leaving my drunk date and me in the living room. I had kissed Jennifer once and was moving in for another kiss, planning how to maneuver her to a bedroom, when she sat up, smacking my nose with her forehead.

"Oh, gosh, I just remembered something about you."

I leaned forward to get things back on track when she screamed, "Marnie! Marnie, come *in* here!"

Nose and ear throbbing, I slumped back into the couch. I figured all chances of losing my virginity were lost, but I didn't know why my date was shrieking.

Marnie appeared, zipping her jeans. "What's wrong?"

"Marnie, do you remember my party in first grade? My birthday, when the clown came and made balloon animals?"

Ah, shit.

Houston was in the doorway now.

"Yeah, what about it?" Marnie asked.

"There was a boy that went all wonky, remember?"

Marnie laughed. "Yeah, he peed his pants and then locked himself in the bathroom. Your mom had to call his mom to come. . . ." She trailed off and looked at me.

My date, now overcome with the giggles, pointed at me, giggled, wiped her eyes, and slapped her knee, occasionally missing the target. Great, not only was I not getting laid. I was getting dissed by someone too drunk to find her own anatomy.

I got up and fished the keys from my pocket. "Help your friend to the car, Marnie."

That time clowns kept Houston from getting laid too.

"Houston, I hate to admit this, but you might be right. 3-D Lisa was a sure thing and the clowns blew it."

"That wasn't the only thing. Remember our campout in fourth grade?" Houston asked.

Houston's dad had pitched a tent in his backyard. We told each other ghost stories in the dark, then climbed into our sleeping bags. Slacker unzipped his, flipped it open to reveal a flannel lining of red and blue stripes and tumbling clowns. My mother had to come pick me up that time too.

"And dinner at my house, March 7, when we were eighth graders?" Slacker told the story like I hadn't been there. "You begged us not to tell anyone about you and the clowns, so I didn't. Not my parents, even. So we're all around the table and Mom comes out with a hot apple cobbler. She's wearing an apron with a big clown face on it and oven mitts that open up in big clown smiles. She reached past you to put the cobbler on the table and the mitt touched you. You garffed your dinner all over the table, Mom, and the cobbler." Slacker shook his head. "Talk about lost opportunities. Mom makes great cobbler."

I sighed. "I gotta get over this," I said.

"Relax, we'll be kind," Boston said. "This is how it works. First we take away this 'I hate clown' madness. That's pure co-dependency." Slacker hefted the duffel and pointed to it like I was too dim to get the connection.

"Then we start introducing clown stuff to you in gradually larger doses. Start small and from far away. I've done research."

"Can't I take two aspirin and stay away from clowns?"

"And how would that have kept you from bailing on Third Date Lisa?" Houston asked.

"Shut up, Houston. There are bigger issues." Boston sounded pissed.

"Slacker, hand it over." Slacker pulled something out of his pocket and passed it to Boston. A little rubber finger puppet. Of a clown.

She put it on her finger. Wiggled it.

My throat tightened. Its nasty red nose nodded toward me, then back. Its painted smile . . . I scrambled off the bed.

"This little clown has been right here in the room the whole time and you've been fine," Boston said.

"If a rattlesnake were here and you didn't know it, you'd be fine until you saw it," I said.

"True," Slacker said. He was nosing through my Palm Pilot. "You've got a dentist appointment next week—you should put a reminder the day before."

"I don't have to—you'll call me. Get that clown out of my face."

Boston took the puppet off her finger. "Fine, here, it's sitting on the windowsill, all the way across the room. It's going to stay there until we leave. It's tiny; you're big. It's inanimate; you can move. You win. Throw it out the window if you want."

"I can't touch it."

"Won't. There's a dif."

I had backed into a corner. Knew I looked incredibly stupid. I took a deep breath. "Okay, fine." I put one foot out, then another. Eyes on the clown. I sat on the bed. Staring at the clown.

"What now?"

"How do you feel?" Boston asked.

I wiped the sweat off my face and swiped it onto her arm.

"Gross," Houston said.

"Demonstrative evidence," Boston said.

Slacker disappeared and came back with a towel.

"End of Part One. Now we leave. But we take the puppet and place it somewhere in the house. You'll know it's there, but not where. You won't see it. You sleep tonight, knowing a little rubber clown is in your house. One you've already conquered. Got that?"

Houston tossed me the football. "Here's to the new Will."

"Oh." This from Slacker. "I already talked to your parents. They won't toss the clown no matter how much you whine."

Busted.

Boston tossed the puppet to Slacker. "Put this some-where. In plain sight. Downstairs."

I flopped back and covered my face with the pillow.

Houston ripped it away. "No suicide attempts. That's taking clown-o-phobia too far."

Boston took the pillow and whacked her twin with it. "Out."

Houston grumbled, but he left.

Boston leaned over me. "This Third Date Lisa thing? It's not about the clowns." She put her middle finger against her thumb and popped me between the eyes.

I listened to music. No luck. I tried to read. Nope. I tried to sleep. My throat and chest were tight, and all because I knew that damn clown lurked in the house. It's not like other people think *cute circus clown* and I think *John Wayne Gacy.* The normal person sees Bozo and I go straight to Pennywise, Insane Clown Posse, and Krusty. It's pure gut. See clown. Brain initiates panic sequence. I tossed and turned. I paced.

I wanted to get with the program. I needed to get past the clown thing. I was the butt of school jokes. Houston had made sure the girls wouldn't joke out loud. The guys wouldn't make them to my face because I was big and valuable on the starting line. But it was there. Wilting Will. Big Baby scared of something a first grader invites to his birthday party. Not good. Not like being allergic to cats. Self-limiting. Fear is something you pass on to your kids. A whole lot of not good.

I could do this.

I roamed the house until I found it. Downstairs. The rarely used formal living room. Coffee table. I stared it down, but I had to back out of the room.

I backed all the way up the stairs and shut my door. I wiped my sweaty palms on the bottom of my tee, then pulled it up and mopped my face.

Finally at midnight, I called my dad's dog. Ruddy is a trained retriever. I pointed to the leering, shit-faced clown. "Fetch it up." Ruddy gave me a questioning glance, then trotted over to the coffee table and seized the puppet in his soft-mouthed carry. He returned to heel. I walked him outside and around the corner. "Drop."

We returned clownless.

And I slept.

The next morning another surprise waited at my locker. Female, cute, not the bony, skinny kind, but the kind of girl who looks like she's always been the catcher for her softball team. The messed-up kind of hair that's supposed to look messed up. Jeans. Tight little tee that teases the waist and dares me to catch sight of a belly button. Oh, please let me see that belly button.

"Hey," she said.

Being totally cool, I said, "Hey."

"I saw what happened yesterday," she said.

Great. She leaned against my locker so I couldn't get my books. I'd look even more like an idiot than ever if I left. Does shame never end? Asteroids. Calling the asteroids.

"I'm not here to . . ." She put up a hand. "I . . . thought you'd like to know you're not the only one."

What? I treated her to my "Duh?" look.

"Clowns. Me too. Freak me out. Can't even see a picture without the skin crawls. For me, hell's got to be a circus."

Tensions I didn't know I had fled my body. "No shit?"

She slid over so I could get into my locker. "Yeah. I know kids that sort of don't like clowns, but it's no big deal. They still function if one wanders by the room. Not me."

"So you *get* it? It's not like when you hate broccoli."

"Sure. How many times have you heard 'Calm down—clowns are funny'?"

I banged my locker shut. "I can't count that high." I looked at her again. "Why don't I know you?"

"Good question," she said. "I'm a sophomore. I guess I'm off your radar. And I don't run with the A-list."

"Meet me for lunch," I said. "We'll go anywhere but—"

"Don't even say it," she said. Real clown phobics never name the burger-slinging evil clown.

The warning bell rang. She pointed over her shoulder. "I go that way. See you later." She sauntered away. I enjoyed the view.

"Hey," I called. "I don't know your name." She stopped and turned.

"Kelli, with an i. A reason to totally disown your parents." She smiled with a dimple that drew my attention up from the now-you-almost-see-it-now-you-don't belly button. "I'm legally changing my name when I'm eighteen."

"Yeah? To what?"

"Debbi. With an *i.*"

Oh yeah, I wanted to marry her and stare at her belly button as full-time employment.

And so five days went by. The intervention team came nightly and brought clown-related objects. I fought nausea and panic and suffocation. I tried to talk myself into ignoring the clown. I tried to believe I was bigger than The Clown. Stronger than The Clown. Smarter than The Clown. But it ended the same. Only after Ruddy fetched, walked, and dropped was my mental health restored.

Then I phoned Kelli and chatted until owl hours. Soon I knew her favorite foods, her most embarrassing moment, why she adored one grandmother and disliked the other, when she learned to tie her shoelaces and who taught her.

She knew, as many did not, that I am called Will because the H. B. in H. B. Williams VI stands for Horace Bertram, and trust money depended on inheriting the name.

"Do daughters inherit anything?"

"Yeah, sure."

"Do they have to be named Horace?"

"Nope."

"Now that's the first time I've felt sorry for the male inheritor."

We went to the movies. We kissed on her front porch. In my car. On her couch. In my dreams.

And then I figured it out.

Finally, I figured it all out.

Boston came in with a rolled-up poster. Slacker had the tape. When she unrolled it and headed for my wall, I took a deep breath and took control.

"Don't."

"Will, this is pretty much the end. Poster on your wall. You look at it every day. Coulrophobia cured."

"No more worries about not getting it because of a clown," Houston said. He tossed me the phone. "Now you can call 3-D Lisa and prove yourself."

"Will, you've been doing great. You've been able to sleep with the other clowns in the house. You've—"

"Been totally lying to you," I said.

Slacker quit organizing my desk. "Huh?"

Boston dropped onto the bed.

"Shit!" Houston said.

"You leave, I call dad's dog, he fetches the clown, clown disappears. I sleep."

"It's Kelli," Houston said. "Boss said she could make you co-dependent."

"Shut up, Houston." Boston again. Slacker organized extra hard.

I tossed the ball to Houston and flopped onto the bed. Boston rerolled the poster.

"Here's the truth," I said. "If Houston were scared of clowns and walked into that room with Lisa, he'd have walked out and found another room, or a car, or a dugout, or a cemetery, any place to close the deal."

I raised my eyebrows. "Right?"

"Damn skippy," Houston said, hoisting the ball over his head to punctuate.

"But I didn't."

Houston looked from me to Boston to Slacker and back to me. "And?"

"So clowns were never the problem."

Boston pumped her fist in the air. "Yes!"

"But you're scared of clowns!" Houston insisted. "Boss, read him that stuff about missed opportunities, about that place that charges all that money to get rid of clown-o-phobia."

"Nobody has ever gone to them to cure coulrophobia," Boston said.

"I need to deal with this clown fear," I said. "I know that. But it didn't interfere with my sex life."

"Sure it did." Houston's face flushed. "You didn't get laid."

"I didn't want to. The clowns were an excuse. Why have sex with a girl who owns a clown collection? It's not the clowns. The question is, Why didn't I know that about her?"

"Who cares?" Houston banged his head with the football. "Slacker, should I throw him out the window or should I jump?"

"Houston," I said. "You're a player—"

"Slut," Boston said.

"Your whole goal is to carry the ball down the field and score. The rush for you is the score. It doesn't matter which football you carry, right?"

"Duh!" Houston agreed.

"It does to me."

"I'm lost," Houston said. "Aren't we talking about clowns?"

"We are," Boston said. "Yup, we certainly are."

Clowns are evil. False happy faces, fake painted smiles, red noses, big feet. Everything oversize and unreal. They make me feel like my eyes lose their logic and the world becomes unknown and unsafe. I just don't like them.

Getting to know a person, slow and easy, finding out that her logic dovetails with mine, that our perspectives line up—now I know that can take my breath away too. It makes my heart race and my palms sweat.

That's a different feeling. And it's not bad. At all.

■ ■ ■

ABOUT THE AUTHOR

Most people think of clowns as funny-looking characters who do silly things. But when Gail Giles taught remedial reading in high school, she was surprised to find that "many teenagers had an abiding fear of clowns. Did not want to see them, read about them, hear about them, and it was more boys than girls who felt that way. Lots of things interest me, but that interested me a lot." And so she chose to write about coulrophobia for this anthology.

After twenty years of teaching teenagers, Gail Giles decided to write novels for them, titling her first book *Shattering Glass*. It was an instant hit, due to the quality of its writing as well as its story line. In the first paragraph of the book, the narrator announces that he and a group of other students killed a fellow student just because they hated him, and then he describes how that all happened. The book was an American Library Association Best Book for Young Adults, an ALA Quick Pick, and a *Booklist* Top Ten Mystery for Youth.

Giles's writing has been called "compelling," "disturbing," and "suspenseful," all of which can be seen in her second novel,

Dead Girls Don't Write Letters, which was a Book Sense 76 Choice, a YALSA Teens Top Ten book, an ALA Quick Pick, and a nominee for the Michigan Thumbs Up! Award.

Gail Giles recently moved from Alaska back to Texas, where she was born and raised. "I'll miss the moose," she says.

Her newest novel is *Playing in Traffic,* another hard-hitting story about a high school senior boy with a dreary life who gets involved with Skye, a pierced, tattooed, and disturbed goth girl who promises Matt an alternative, exciting, and dangerous lifestyle characterized by drugs and sex.

. . .

If you are claustrophobic, you may need . . .

Instructions for Tight Places
. . . . .
Kelly Easton

Don't Scream: It could happen anywhere. You could be on the elevator, say, going down, down, down. You have to get to school *somehow,* and you live on the 33rd floor. You get in and face toward the back wall, close your eyes. It's cool. No problem. Just that wonderful sensation of being trapped in a tube plummeting through space. You're alone, but by, like, floor number 28, they start to crush in. Even facing the other way, you know them by smell.

There's Mrs. Raintree with her crippled poodle, its back legs propped on a little skateboard apparatus. Floor 27, and it's the super with his T-shirt and hairy armpits, like this was the Bronx rather than the Upper East Side. On 26, 25, 24, the working stiffs crowd in, their cologne as choking as formaldehyde.

Take deep breaths: All you're trying to do is get to school. It shouldn't be this hard. Your backpack is a recipe for osteoporosis and skeletal degeneration. But you leave it on, its massive weight a wedge between you and the others. You wish you had your cello for further protection, that it was a day for Ms. Gucci's "Strings and Things."

Still, you're surviving, keeping cool. But on floor 20, the Chinese lady with the lilac perfume gets in with her hyper kid. He drops his ball, jolts and shoves to retrieve it, bangs his head against said backpack. And you think, *Chimney, can of sardines, phone booth, coffin.* You think, *Tall buildings are not safe anymore.* The smell of dog dander, hairy armpit sweat, leather, perfume, and old age chokes off your breath. You start to pant like a lady going through hard labor, Lamaze. Sweat flows down your face, like a fly crawling on a horse's back. The tail swats at it, but it's out of reach.

Find someone to talk to: Your best friend, Began, has tried to crack the code of your anxiety. Her name is pronounced bay-GHAN. You're best friends because on her first day at school, when Cecil Harter made fun of her sari, you stepped on his shoelace and sent him sprawling. Even riddled with anxiety, you are one tough cookie, fight or flight, adrenaline speeding to the ends of your nerves like cars racing to the finish line.

Began scolded you, though. Said, "There was no need for that," sounding like Mahatma Gandhi.

"No, there wasn't," you admitted, "but it sure was fun."

She smiled. "Come over to my house," she said in her spacious dialect.

"How many flights up is it?" you asked.

"Flights?"

"Elevator stops?"

"None. No, it is flat. A house."

That was five years ago. She no longer wears saris or speaks as if there's a stop sign between every word. She wears Gap jeans and Abercrombie shirts and Nikes. Her lunch box is still filled with samosas, garlic nan, and chutney, though.

Still, she's loyal. When you have one of your . . . *attacks,* Began looks at you with her deep eyes and goes, "What is the origin of this problem?"

You shrug. You weren't kept in a shoebox as a baby, or locked in a closet. Your parents are just raising you in the wrong place!

"It must be *something,*" she goes, because Began is going to be a psychiatrist like her dad, the talking rather than the drugging kind, so she knows there's a *root* to everything. "Something from the past?" she goes. And she's Indian, after all, so when she refers to the past, she could mean, like, previous *lives.*

"I don't remember."

She nods, wisely. She could be barfing and look spiritual. "Classic. You're blocking it."

Remind yourself you're in control: You did scream once, a couple of years back, in the elevator with all the bodies in it, shrieked in a way that had them ducking like you were packing a weapon rather than a musical instrument in your case. Mrs. Raintree stabbed the emergency button with her hand. The elevator slammed to a halt. Mr. Ferris, who is older than God and can't see, fell to the floor.

The screaming had made things *worse;* in other words, it didn't solve the problem. Later, your dad, who believes in *civil responsibility* and *accountability for one's deeds,* brought you round to each and every inhabitant's apartment for you to apologize. They all stared at you, scientifically, microscopically, and said nothing, except Mrs. Raintree, who patted your shoulder and said, "I understand, dear. I have an anxiety disorder too. Xanax works wonders."

Become a spot on the floor: It's not just in the elevator that it happens. You could be in a department store at Christmastime, the shoppers more willing to commit an act of violence than give up that discounted Gucci bag.

You could be in the park watching the kids lined up and shoving at the slide, or crowding into the tube that looks like a drainage pipe. You could be walking down the street during rush hour or strapped into the dentist's chair.

Or you could be at school. When the bell rings between classes and the students flood the hall, you feel like the Egyptians chasing the Jews into the Red Sea. If you'll remember, God parted said sea for the Jews, but when the Egyptians followed, they were drowned.

"It's a giant grave," you tell Began, tiring of ocean metaphors. "Like Poe or something. We're all, like, knocking on the casket, *Let me out,* only it's our own hearts beating."

"I don't think the story goes like that. And no one else feels that," Began reasons.

"Okay, maybe not Poe. It's . . . India, the streets of New Delhi jammed with bodies. There are beggars and lepers, or beggars who are lepers. One of them puts out his hand for a coin and there are no fingertips. And you're like, 'For God's sake, antibiotics can cure this.'"

"Yes, India is crowded," Began sighs. "But it feels so natural when you're there. Like a river of people. Like water flowing."

She says things like that.

"Okay. Okay. Sorry about the India part," you go. "I get carried away a little."

"A little?"

"The problem is not in me," you argue. "It's the

outside world. Remember that soccer match in Italy where, like, all these English guys shoved the fence onto the Italian fans and crushed them. Or that kid in the movie theater fire who fell on the floor and got trampled."

"His mother should have taken him with her," she scolds.

"The Twin Towers," you go, saving the worst for last, although the panic was there before then, even before then.

"This is very bad." She shakes her head.

And you wonder: *Does, she mean* terrorism, bad? *Or me,* bad?

"We will try meditation," she offers.

"Why not?" you agree. You've tried everything else. There was a series of shrinks, hypnosis, biofeedback, breathing exercises, an audiotape of pebbles dropping supplied by Ms. Gucci, medication that made you so drowsy you fell asleep in ceramics, the clay splatting on the wheel.

Think of alternatives: It's not like you didn't try the stairs. The thirty-three flights equal about 300 calories burned, you figured, so you approached the task with something close to enthusiasm.

But then Mrs. Raintree and her fellow dog-owners decided that in winter the stairs were, well, they were the great outdoors. The occasional puddle became the chronic pile, the stench resembling the strike of the garbage workers. And you're pretty sure a few drunken singles added their contributions so that even the vast stairwell felt like being locked in a portable potty.

Remember a pleasant occasion, such as a birthday party or a field trip: There are days when you forget about closed spaces, and life opens up like a massive stadium after a game. Like the rainy day when you took the Staten Island Ferry with Jason. It was empty except for a couple of nuns under black umbrellas, and Jason turned you away from the rail, toward him, said your hair reminded him of cotton candy or taffy, something sticky, then he kissed you. Or when you forget yourself in the cello, fall into the music like a parachutist, rather than playing (Ms. Gucci says) as if you are "being chased by a swarm of bees."

Go to your quiet place: Saturday morning, Began comes to your apartment. She unrolls a little rug, lights a candle and incense. Together, you sit in the lotus position and try to empty your minds. "Focus on a spot on the floor," she goes.

"Been there. Done that."

"Then just close your eyes."

You close your eyes for a second, then open them. You study your feet, the candle, Began, and the calendar on your wall. Your thoughts crash through your head like a rioting mob. You wonder why the days are marked by squares instead of circles, as if to demarcate their finiteness. Why can't time be round, or an ocean, or an elephant, who never forgets? Then you wonder why Jason now looks away from you in the hall, or why your mom stays up all night smoking at the kitchen table while your dad sacks out in front of CNN. But you don't tell Began. Her face is too calm and hopeful. Instead, you instruct her to come every Saturday, and she agrees. You'll give meditation a try.

Get real: One thing you do know is that when you screamed in the elevator, or panicked on Madison Avenue and curled into a ball on the sidewalk, you felt less minute, more in control. Your mom had been stopped by the super on her way to work, and she had to call in sick while she searched the yellow pages for a psychiatrist. Your dad took a taxi from Wall Street, unfurled your body, and escorted you home like a guide dog.

Both times you felt more like a *something* rather than a speck of dust in a pile. It's like your fear gave you shape, definition.

Empty your mind: After a few weeks of meditation, you notice something: as soon as Began walks into your room, your mind unclenches just a tad. Your breath slows.

It isn't a cure. It's just a loosening in your chest, as if a cat is unwinding a ball of yarn there.

Began bows and sits silently on the rug. Instead of trying to go blank canvas, you direct your mind to one of the places you will move to when you grow up: the Alaskan tundra, the Dakota Badlands, the Texas desert. The problem is outside of you, and outside will have to change.

Began's breath is like lapping water. The incense smells like trees. A prairie arises in your mind, flat and far and horizonless. You stand there by yourself, under the vast, open sky, watching snow fall lightly from the sky.

■ ■ ■

ABOUT THE AUTHOR

With degrees in theater and playwriting from the University of California, Kelly Easton became a member of the faculty at the University of North Carolina at Wilmington, where she coordinated the internship program in creative writing. After publishing short stories for adults in various literary journals and winning first prize in the North Carolina Writers' Network 1997 Fiction Competition, she turned her attention to writing novels for middle graders and young adults.

For readers eight to twelve years old, she has published a pair of comical mysteries about a boy who lives in a pet store: *Trouble at Betts Pets* and *Canaries and Criminals*. Her first novel for young adults, *The Life History of a Star*, is about a sarcastic teenage girl in the 1970s dealing with problems of growing up, while worrying about her older brother who lives in the attic after returning from the Vietnam War physically and emotionally damaged. That novel won a Golden Kite Honor, was named a Top Ten Book for Teens by Book Sense 76, and was an American Library Association Popular Paperback for Teens. Her second young adult novel was *Walking on Air,* the story of a twelve-year-old tightrope walker who performs in the religious revival shows run by her preacher father during the Great Depression.

Kelly Easton, who lives with her two children in Rhode Island, knows what she's talking about in "Instructions for Tight Places" because she herself is claustrophobic. "Although not to the extent of my character," she says. She also admits to being "very overwhelmed by crowds." She solves that by avoiding them.

Her newest young adult novels are *Three Witches and a Wart* and *Definitions.*

• • •

Every student at Bleakhaven Academy is terrified of something.
So why is Gavin there?

Fear-for-All

· · · · ·

Neal Shusterman

The headmistress had eyes that didn't quite focus on yours. That's what Gavin first noticed. Miss Olivette was looking straight at him, but wasn't. It was as if her focus was off by just a few inches, like she was looking at a point somewhere in the middle of his brain.

"If you're trying to intimidate me, it's not working," Gavin said. "I'm not afraid of you."

The tight-skinned, tightlipped woman only smiled. Her smile was like a clean slice of a bloodless wound. "Then what are you afraid of?"

"Nothing," he answered, without hesitation. He'd had guidance counselors asking him that question for years, and the answer never changed. Of course no one believed him. Everyone was always so sure he was posturing, concealing some fear so deep he was afraid to utter it. They could not accept the possibility of a kid who was born afraid of nothing. Not pain, not death, not retribution for his actions. Perhaps the very concept of him frightened them.

"I want to know why you accepted me into this school."

The bloodless grin never left Miss Olivette's face. "Why? Don't you feel you deserve to attend Bleakhaven Academy?"

"No, I don't. My grades are lousy, my attitude stinks, I've already been thrown out of two high schools—and yet you've given me a full scholarship. Why?"

"Let's have a look at your record, shall we?" She flipped open a fat folder on her desk.

"Last year you took an acrophobic student to the roof of your school and forced him to look down from the edge."

"Yeah," Gavin said, shifting in his seat. "I got expelled for that."

She flipped a page. "Six months ago you hit the stop button in an elevator when you found out the woman next to you was claustrophobic."

"Yeah. She sure freaked."

"And we have a letter from one Myra O'Dell, claiming you terrorized her by taking her on a date to the circus."

"C'mon—it was just the circus."

"Did you know she was coulrophobic?"

"You mean afraid of clowns?" Gavin shrugged. "Yeah, I knew."

The headmistress closed the folder gently. "People believe you did these things to be cruel. That you're a horrible, evil child." She paused to let it sink in. "Are you?"

Gavin looked away from her, hating her eyes. He could almost feel those eyes like laser beams converging on some spot in his brain, burning it away like you might burn away a tumor.

Was he evil? Was he cruel? Surely those things he had done were cruel—but somehow at the time they didn't feel that way.

"Why did you do those things?" the headmistress demanded.

"I don't know!" he answered. But that wasn't entirely true. There was a part of him that did know, but only in the most glancing of ways. The way a ship's lookout knew the iceberg.

"I did it because I wanted to . . . understand." It was the only way he could put those feelings into words. That compulsion he felt to go to the roof, or to stop that elevator, or to coldly observe his screaming date there in the front row as the wire-haired, white-faced clown ran around and around. He had never jumped from an unexpected fright. He had never experienced terror. How could he help but find himself drawn to those who did? And in the end, his date stopped screaming, didn't she? So maybe he had actually done something good. Wasn't that possible?

When Gavin met the headmistress's eyes again, she seemed very satisfied with herself. And with him as well.

"So, did you?"

"Did I what?"

"You said you wanted to understand. Did you?"

Gavin thought back to the instances when he had sparked another's fear. Did he understand it? Perhaps for an instant, when their fear was so overpowering it surrounded them both. For just the tiniest instant in time he could wrap it around him like a cloak, almost feeling it—but it would only surround him, never penetrating. Then it would dissolve so quickly he could never be sure if he had felt anything at all.

"No," he told her. It was easier than trying to explain. Yet somehow he felt she needed no explanation.

"You never answered my question," Gavin said, beginning to lose his limited patience. "If I'm such a 'bad seed,' then why am I here?"

The headmistress slowly crossed her fingers before her. Her interlaced hands looked like a pale spider patiently awaiting its prey.

"You're here because you possess a quality that we here at Bleakhaven value above all else."

"What?"

And then she leaned forward and whispered so low that it was just at the threshold of hearing, but with such intensity, it could have knocked Gavin out of his chair.

"Fearlessness."

His roommate was a football player. A big kid. The kind of guy who would beat up weird, weaselly kids like Gavin.

"That's your side of the room," the kid told him, as if it wasn't obvious. "Hope you like country music, 'cause I play it all the time."

"Country's okay," Gavin said. "if you can put up with some rap."

"Not a problem."

Only after the music issue was settled did his roommate introduce himself. "I'm Parker," he said. "Parker Van der Meek."

"Van der Meek," Gavin repeated. "Easy to remember. Just like that senator."

"Yeah," said Parker. "He's my dad."

Gavin snapped his eyes up, to check if Parker was kidding, but he wasn't.

"Yeah," said Parker. "A lot of bigwigs send their 'high-needs' kids to this school."

"'High needs'? Like 'special needs'?"

"Hell no!" said Parker. "'Special needs' is learning disabilities and stuff like that. 'High needs' is . . . well . . . other stuff."

Gavin would have asked what "other stuff" he meant, but he could tell Parker just wasn't gonna go there.

Gavin began to unpack his suitcase, and then he realized Parker was staring at him. It annoyed him, so he said, "You wanna help me unpack?"

"No, that's okay," said Parker. "So, you're the one they've been talking about? The one who's getting a free ride."

"Yeah. So?"

"Nothing. It's just that Miss Olivette keeps telling us we gotta treat you good. She says you're very important to all of us."

Gavin couldn't figure out why he'd be important to anyone, least of all to a senator's kid. "She's one weird witch," Gavin said.

He pulled back his linen to make his bed, and there between the sheets sat a cockroach. A big one, like the kind you get at the end of summer. Gavin laughed. "Hey, Parker—you think this roach knows he's going to one of the most exclusive schools in the country?"

But Parker wasn't answering. Gavin turned to see his roommate backed into the corner of his bed, hands spread out against the wall—his jaw locked and eyes peeled so far back it was as if he had no eyelids.

"S-st-step on it!" Parker hissed. "K-ki-kill it. Kill it now. *Now, now, now.*"

His breath came in such short, tight bursts, Gavin could swear the kid was having a heart attack. He had seen this look before. He had seen it in an elevator. He had seen it on a rooftop. He had seen it at the Greatest Show on Earth.

"K-k-kill it. Pleeeeeheehees . . ."

Gavin looked down at the roach. It wasn't moving very quickly to escape, probably because it was so fat.

"Kill it . . . Pleeeese . . . I'm entomophobic. I have a fear of bugs—you have to kill it!"

"What, this?" Gavin picked up the roach and took a step toward Parker with the roach in his upturned palm. Parker gasped and pressed deeper into the corner. If he could, Gavin knew Parker would disappear right into that corner.

"C'mon, it's just a cockroach." Gavin took one step closer.

Parker was pale, sweating. *"No. Don't!"*

Gavin took another step, and Parker let loose a wail of hopelessness.

For the longest moment, Gavin just stood there. The urge to hold that stupid bug right up to Parker's face was overwhelming. His terror was so intense, so out of control, and yet Gavin couldn't feel it. He could see it. He could smell the fear, but not feel it. *If his fear becomes strong enough, I will,* said a little voice deep in Gavin's mind. *Bring that bug to him, set it on the tip of his nose. Make his terror so powerful that some of it will sink into me, too. Then I'll feel it. Then I'll know.*

Gavin closed his eyes. No. He wouldn't do it. If only because Parker was his roommate and he had to deal with him all year. Gavin fought down that irresistible urge to cultivate Parker's fear and instead hurled the roach out the window.

Parker relaxed immediately. A breeze blew through the window. It was as if the room itself was breathing a sigh of relief.

"Thanks, man," Parker said. "Thanks. Really. Thanks."

Then he reached out and grabbed Gavin's arm. Gavin didn't know what it was, but there was something weird about that moment. It made all the hairs on his arm stand on end.

He pulled away from Parker's grip. "No problem."

Gavin very quickly came to understand exactly what Parker had meant by "high needs."

At lunch, Parker introduced him to a table full of other students. Melissa was the daughter of a software billionaire. Barth's mother was the lieutenant governor, and although no one knew what Daniel's parents did, the family was rumored to be "richer than God on Good Friday," as Parker put it. Everything seemed fine, until Gavin got up to get a knife to cut his steak. Parker grabbed him by the wrist, pulled him back down, and quietly said, "Don't."

"Huh?"

"Just don't."

As Gavin tried to process this strange request, he noticed that no one at the table had steak knives—or any knives, for that matter. There were no forks, either. Only spoons—and plastic ones at that. Then, when Gavin looked around, he saw that every other table had kids eating with silverware, not cheap cafeteria stuff, either, but real, polished silver—the kind his mother kept locked away in the china hutch. At his table, however, the kids were picking up the steak with their hands and biting into it.

"What's the problem? You guys werewolves or something?"

They just looked at him blankly, as if maybe they really were.

"I mean—do you have a problem with silver? You know—silver bullets, silverware?"

They looked at one another, then looked away as if Gavin had said something unspeakable. Finally Parker spoke up. "Melissa has belonephobia."

"Fear of sharp objects," Melissa explained. "Knives, forks, and scissors, mostly."

Gavin let out a single guffaw of laughter. He hadn't meant to; it just came out.

Melissa narrowed her eyes. "You think that's funny?"

Gavin looked at those angry eyes and felt himself getting angry right back. "I don't know. Maybe. Don't you think it's funny?"

"Hey, he's new!" said Parker, jumping in. "Give him a break."

"The truth is," said Daniel, "we've all got some phobia."

"Everyone at the table?" said Gavin.

"No," Daniel answered. "Everyone at the school. That's why we're here. That's Bleakhaven's specialty."

"You mean, you didn't know?" said Melissa, as if she felt sorry for him somehow.

Gavin looked around at the other tables. There were no signs of anything unusual, but then a phobia wasn't really something you wore on your sleeve. It was very personal. Very hidden. That is, until the moment the fear took over.

"I have catoptrophobia," whispered Barth. "That's a fear of mirrors."

Then Daniel pointed to himself almost as a matter of pride. "I'm afraid of numbers divisible by three," he said. "They don't even have a name for that!"

Gavin just stared at him, gaping.

"It's true. If there were six people at this table, I would have to leave."

Gavin found himself stuttering, "But that's just dumb! It doesn't even make sense."

Daniel shrugged. "Of course it doesn't make sense," he said. "It's irrational. A phobia is an irrational fear."

"If it made sense," said Melissa, a little bit of anger still in her voice, "we'd be able to do something about it, wouldn't we?"

"Nikola Tesla was afraid of numbers divisible by three," said Daniel. "And he was a great scientist!"

"So how about you?" Barth asked. "What are you afraid of?"

There it was. That question again. He was getting so tired of that question.

"Nothing."

"He's lying," snapped Melissa. "Everyone's here for a reason."

Gavin didn't answer her. Instead, he looked down at his steak, then reached into his pocket and pulled out the Swiss Army knife he always carried. Usually he just used it to clip his nails. Today it would serve another function.

"Wh-what are you doing?" Melissa asked, her voice already beginning to tremble.

"I'm cutting my meat. You have a problem with that?" And then he pulled out the blade, plunging it into the meat.

The reaction was instantaneous. Melissa stood up so quickly, her chair flew out behind her, her hands started to shake uncontrollably, and she let loose a banshee screech that brought silence to the rest of the dining room. All the while Gavin kept eye contact with her. She tried to look away, but her eyes were glued on Gavin and that knife.

The others got up to help her. Parker reached over, took the knife away, and Melissa just about collapsed in Daniel's and Barth's arms once it was out of sight.

"Nice going, idiot," Parker said, and slipped the knife into his own pocket, to make sure Gavin didn't try it again. Silence still ruled the room, and Gavin caught the eyes of the headmistress glaring down at him from the faculty table. No, not glaring . . . studying.

Melissa, who had gone white as the tablecloth, was now turning as red as Gavin's rare steak. She strode over to him, pulled her hand way back, and slapped him so hard across the face, his head practically spun around.

And in that instant that her palm touched his face, he felt something. More than just the sting of the slap; it was something intense and dark. It raised goose flesh all over his body, just like Parker's touch had earlier. He couldn't explain it—but that was the feeling he remembered long after the sting of the slap was gone.

Gavin sat alone at dinner, marveling at how quickly he was able to alienate himself from these kids. Why did he always do that? He chuckled bitterly to himself, wondering if perhaps he had a phobia after all. A fear of friendship. *What would that be called?* he wondered. *Comradophobia? Palophobia?* Gavin supposed there were as many phobias as there were things in the world to be afraid of. Still, he knew that a fear of friendship was not his problem.

It was embarrassing to have the big round table all to himself in the midst of a crowded dining hall, so he tried not to meet eyes with anyone. Still, there were some things he couldn't help but notice. Like the way Miss Olivette watched him from the faculty table. Or the way his roommate worked the room, whispering to other students and pointing at Gavin. Or the way Melissa, the girl who had slapped him, was eating a thick lamb chop with a knife and fork.

Gavin had chosen a hamburger tonight. He couldn't quite say why.

"I want out of here." Gavin paced across the fancy Persian carpets of Miss Olivette's huge office. "I don't care if it's free. I don't even care if the next stop is juvie—I want out."

Miss Olivette sat calmly in her high-backed leather chair studying him, always studying him. The headmistress seemed neither surprised nor bothered, which only enraged Gavin more.

"Call my parents," Gavin demanded. "I want you to call them now."

But she did not lift a finger to pick up her phone.

"Tell me, Gavin," she said calmly, "in your opinion, what is the opposite of fear?"

"Why are you asking a stupid question? I don't want to answer your stupid questions."

"If you want to go home, you must answer my questions, stupid or not."

Gavin pounded his fist on the desk. Miss Olivette didn't even flinch. "Fine. The opposite of fear is bravery. Are you happy?"

Miss Olivette shook her head. "That's a common misconception," she told him. "Bravery is a *reaction* to fear. Fight or flight. Those are the reactions to a fearful situation. Those who fight are called brave," she said. And then, after a moment of thought, "Or foolhardy, depending on the outcome."

"Why are you telling me this?" Gavin asked. "Why does any of this matter?"

"Now, *there's* a question you'll soon be able to answer for yourself," she said, throwing him a flash of that terrible grin. "I see you've been spending some time with your roommate, Parker. Are you two getting along?"

"No," said Gavin. "I don't like him. I don't like any of them. They're weird."

This affected Miss Olivette more than anything else he'd said. She sat up slightly straighter in her chair. He could feel her bristling like a static charge.

"Tolerance is a virtue, Gavin," she said, her voice just a tiny bit louder than before. "Heaven knows, many people have gone through great pains to tolerate you. A phobia does *not* make a person weird. I have more respect for the kids here than any others—and you should, too."

"Do I get to go home, or not?" Gavin said, wishing he could melt this woman with the anger from his eyes.

"If that's what you want, then you shall go home," Miss Olivette said simply. "But first, there's something I wish to show you."

Then she reached into a lower drawer and pulled out a small cardboard box, just large enough to fit in the palm of her hand. "Our science lab has some very interesting specimens. Have you been down there yet?"

Gavin shook his head. "What's in the box?" he asked.

"A gift," said Miss Olivette. "Something special, something just for you." She opened the lid of the box.

At first it appeared empty, and then two tiny antennae wiggled into view, followed by the body of a beetle, shiny and green. . . .

And Gavin was struck by a sensation so foreign, so unexpected, it stole the very air from his lungs. He felt himself moving backward, even though he hadn't told his feet to move. His eyes were locked on the bug, like somehow it controlled him. His chest tightened. His throat swelled so that he couldn't breathe, and he heard himself squeaking out rasping gasps as he tried to get air.

What was this? What was this feeling? His mind reeled, trying to comprehend its intensity. It was ruthless. It was vicious, like a thousand knives slicing through his brain, his heart, his guts. And still the beetle peered at him from the lip of the box, wiggling its horrible antennae.

Gavin found himself in the very corner of the room, squeezing into that corner, trying to disappear. And Miss Olivette approached with the beetle in the palm of her hand. As she did, the feeling only grew worse.

"Make it stop," squealed Gavin. *"Please, make it stop."*

"When you first came to my office," she said in that calm, calm voice of hers, "you told me you wanted to understand. Now do you understand?"

It took all of Gavin's will to make his head nod up and down. This was fear; he knew that now. This was what others felt. It was like a gash across his soul, making the very essence of his life vulnerable. How could anyone live with this?

"Please," he said, his voice just a whisper. *"Please, stop it."*

In one smooth motion, Miss Olivette dropped the bug to the floor and crushed it beneath her shiny black shoe, grinding it back and forth until there was nothing left of it. In a moment the fear was gone. The sensation that flowed through Gavin now was as powerful and as unexpected as the first. He felt his throat opening, the pores of his body opening. Air flooded into his lungs. Satisfied relief numbed his brain like a drug.

"Thank you" was all he could say. "Thank you."

He sat there in the corner, regaining his strength, relishing the depth of his own relief.

"Now then," said Miss Olivette, "tell me: what is the opposite of fear?"

And he gave her the answer that everyone else who attended Bleakhaven Academy already knew.

"Peace." He told her. "The opposite of fear is peace."

The headmistress offered him a satisfied grin. "Very, very good! Now, it's time for you to go. There is a special assembly this evening, and you must get yourself ready."

Gavin slowly lifted his head as if it weighed more than his neck could sustain. "Assembly?"

"Yes. You mustn't miss it."

"I want to go home. You said I could go home."

"Of course," she said. The calm in her voice was meant to soothe but rinsed over Gavin like ice water. "But first the assembly. Your roommate is here to accompany you back to your room."

Gavin turned to see Parker waiting at the door. He had no idea how long Parker had been there, or how much he had seen.

Parker looked at him oddly—Gavin could not remember anyone ever looking at him in this particular way. Was it pity? No, that wasn't it.

"C'mon, Gavin," Parker said.

Gavin fought a battle to pull his emotions together and won, although when he stood, his legs felt weak, as if he were on the verge of fever. He could barely even feel his feet as he moved through the door and down the dark cherry-wood hallways of the school. All the while Parker kept sneaking sideways glances at Gavin, the way one might when escorting a celebrity, and it finally occurred to Gavin, exactly the way Parker had been looking at him back in Miss Olivette's office. It was awe. Parker had been awestruck.

"I—I don't know how to thank you," Parker said.

"For what?"

Parker didn't answer. Instead he said, "I went outside this afternoon. I took a walk through the rose garden."

"How nice for you," snapped Gavin. "Did you pick a bouquet for your football coach?"

He expected some rude comment back from Parker, but Parker didn't take the bait.

"You don't understand," he said. "The rose garden is full of bees. There are spider webs stretched between the bushes. I don't go to the rose garden. But now I can." He hesitated for a moment. "I don't know how to thank you."

"Then don't," said Gavin, trying his best to block the image of an insect-filled garden from his mind.

As they turned the corner toward the dormitories, several kids who had been chattering and laughing in the hall stopped and looked at him with that strange gaze of awe. Then they began whispering to one another. *That's him!*" "*He's the one.*" "*Go shake his hand.*" "*I won't do it— you do it!*"

Then a boy stepped forward. He wore a surgical mask, and above the blue edge of the paper mask floated a pair of bulging eyes that were pleading with such intensity,

Gavin could swear those eyes were about ready to pop out of his face. The boy wore latex surgical gloves on his hands, too, making his pale skin appear that much paler. With a deep breath, the boy reached to his right wrist, peeled the glove off with a snap, and thrust his trembling fingers forward.

"I'm Theo. Pleased to meet you."

Gavin had no intention of shaking his hand, but Parker grabbed Gavin's wrist and guided his hand into Theo's until they met, clasping like train couplers. That strange flash of something not-quite-electrical shot from Theo to Gavin, up his arm, to his spine. Synapses fired along his central nervous system, shooting up through the base of his neck into the deepest, most primitive part of his brain. Gavin gasped.

"Germs! You're afraid of germs!"

But Theo pulled off his surgical mask and dropped it, along with both gloves, to the floor. "Not anymore."

Gavin could feel the walls of the hallway begin to squirm. Germs were everywhere. There in the corners. There on the hands and in the breath of all the kids around him. Everything, everyone was so unclean. He looked at his own hands. He would have to scrub and scrub and scrub them until every last germ was gone. How could anyone stand it?

Gavin had to get away from there. Away from *them.* He bolted, and although Parker tried to stop him, Gavin pushed past him, moving with the adrenaline speed of someone fighting for his life, not knowing where he could possibly go, but knowing that he had to leave. He found himself in a stairwell, and, hearing voices beneath him, he climbed up and up, until the stairs were gone, and a ladder went up through a small hole. He took the ladder and found himself in the school's bell tower. The school's massive bells hung above him; the immense bronze shells, blackened from age, held just a hint of their former metallic sheen.

As a fear of heights was not one of his newly adopted terrors, he had no problem going to the edge of the open-air belfry and collapsing on the ledge. He turned his face to the stone pillar beside him, refusing to look out over a world that suddenly seemed so choked with unknown terrors.

He felt sure someone would follow him, to drag him back down to the school, but no one came at first. Then finally he heard a voice. Ice water. But this time, with his thoughts so furiously aflame, that voice was soothing.

"I know what you feel," Miss Olivette said. "I understand, but I can never share it. There are many terrors that have passed through these halls, but they live within the students that come here. I can sympathize with their pain, but never share it. No one can. No one but you."

"Home," Gavin hissed. "You promised."

And with that, she dropped some pages before him. It was a legal document bearing his name and signed by several people. Two of the signatures he recognized as his parents'.

"As you know, we offered you a full scholarship, worth more money than your parents could ever possibly afford . . . but the scholarship required that they sign over all their legal rights."

Gavin raised his eyes to look at her.

"You have been legally adopted by Bleakhaven Academy." She pulled back the document from him. "So you see . . . you *are* home."

"No . . ."

Then she did something Gavin did not expect. She sat beside him on the ledge and took him in her arms. And he allowed it, for in this awful moment, even the embrace of a spider was better than no embrace at all.

"The bells have not rung here for more than ten years," she told him, her voice no longer ice to him, for he had grown accustomed to its chill. "Do you know why?"

Gavin shook his head.

"They haven't rung, because we haven't had someone like you for ten years. There are few in the world like you, and we are honored to count you among our own."

Few like me, he thought. What did that mean? All his life he felt he was somehow different from others around him. The steeled fearlessness that dominated his life, the apparent cruelty with which he treated others. He had longed to be like others — to feel what they felt. Yet even now, as he was truly feeling their innermost pains, he was not becoming like them. He was becoming something else. "What's happening to me?"

Miss Olivette answered with ease, as if the answer was obvious. "You are becoming fear," she said. "You shall be fear, the way our good Lord is sin. You have a solemn duty here. A holy duty. Your panophobia shall be a blessing."

"I don't understand."

"I think you do."

She was right. No matter how much he tried to deny it, he understood. He was a sponge for the terrors that filled every corner of Bleakhaven. As a sponge begins hard and abrasive, so had he been all his life. Without even knowing it, he had been waiting his whole life for this dark purpose.

Tears now poured from his eyes with such intensity his head began to pound. "I can't do this. I can't *be* this. It's more than I can stand."

"Oh, you'll stand it," said Miss Olivette with complete confidence, "because you are strong. And soon you will come to know how much you truly want it."

"Want it?"

"We are never given a gift without the passion to use it."

Gavin reached down into himself to see if this was true, but his thoughts and emotions were so shredded by the storm within him, he had no way of telling.

"I'm scared." It was the one emotion he was sure of.

Until arriving here, he hadn't known what that meant. Now he wished he never had.

"I know," Miss Olivette said, still embracing him. "So many of us spend our lives trying to find our place in the world . . . but I envy you, Gavin, because you know yours. There is nothing more fulfilling than knowing what you are."

"I . . . I am . . . I am fear," he said, trying it on like a strange set of clothes, only to find that it fit. Perfectly. "I am fear for all." His voice felt a bit stronger now. Sturdier. Hearing the strength come back to his own voice brought some strength to the rest of him as well. "They *need* me," he said, realizing that it was true. "More than anything else in the world, they need me."

"Yes!" Miss Olivette said, stroking his hair like a mother. "Thanks to you, they will overcome the fears that hold them back. They will become great leaders, because of you."

"They will remember me."

"They will love you."

"Because I matter."

"More than you know."

Gavin stood, looking out over the grounds and the fields beyond the school. Insects and germs and sharp objects—all these things were out there, striking painfully against his soul, but Miss Olivette was right. No matter how awful the phobias felt, he was strong. He could bear it. Because it was his purpose.

The bells above slowly began to swing, until the clappers hit their mark. The powerful tolls, deafening and resonant, rattled him to the bone, and when they were done, he turned to Miss Olivette, his ears still ringing long after the bells had fallen silent. "The special assembly?"

"The bells have called the students to the great hall. You are the honored guest," she said. "Are you ready?"

I'll never be ready, thought Gavin, *but then, who is ever ready to accept their fate?* "Yes," he said.

I have a purpose, he kept telling himself as he descended from the bell tower. *It is noble. It is good. Imagine me chosen for something good!*

Two students, who barely had the courage to look upon him, swung open the doors of the great hall for Gavin as he and Miss Olivette approached. The vaulted ceiling of the great hall towered before him, full of stained-glass windows and Gothic arches. The rows of seats were packed with students. A single aisle ran down the center of the hall, toward the stage. There was no podium on that stage, for what was to occur here would happen in the aisle. Even now the crowds of students were standing in the rows, pressing toward that center aisle, ready to reach out their hands toward him.

There was a sanctity to this mission. A holiness that would wash him clean, even in the face of his newfound terrors. Panophobia. The fear of all things. It would soon be his cross to bear, and the knowledge that somehow he would bear it gave him the strength he needed to take that first step toward his desperate schoolmates.

With his hands held out wide on either side of him, he began his journey down the aisle like a bridegroom toward the altar, embracing the knowledge that soon he would be very, very afraid.

■ ■ ■

ABOUT THE AUTHOR

Reviewers have called Neal Shusterman's writing "spellbinding," "haunting," "provocative," "stunning," "inventive," "gritty," and "riveting." Most of all, his books are entertaining, whether they are realistic books, true stories, action/adventure, fantasy, or science fiction. Among his award-winning books are *What Daddy Did, The Shadow Club, The Dark Side of Nowhere, Scorpion Shards, Thief of Souls, Shattered Sky, Kid Heroes, The Eyes of Kid Midas, Downsiders, Full Tilt,* and *The Schwa Was Here,* as well as several collections of short stories: *MindQuakes, MindStorms, MindTwisters, MindBenders,* and *Darkness Creeping.* Under the name of Easton Royce, he is also the author of several *X-Files* novelizations.

In addition to books, he has written music, stage plays, and screenplays for films and television, including *Pixel Perfect,* which was one of the Disney Channel's most successful TV movies, and *Downsiders,* which is being made into a TV movie for Disney. As if that were not enough variety, he has also created a series of role-playing games for teens, *How to Host a Teen Mystery,* and another for adults, *How to Host a Murder.*

"When considering which phobia I would write about," Neal Shusterman says, "I found myself most intrigued by the two extremes: a complete absence of fear, set against a fear of everything. So the question was, How to take someone with a complete lack of fear and then take that character on a journey that would leave him or her panophobic. What would someone who was truly fearless be like? The more I thought about it, the more I realized that true fearlessness would be its own handicap, and someone who couldn't experience fear would be emotionally crippled. Therefore, more than anything else in the world, he would want to understand what it meant to be afraid. The true challenge was not just to make that character afraid but to have the character dutifully accept all the fear the world had to offer." The result was "Fear-for-All."

. . .

ABOUT THE EDITOR

A recipient of the ALAN Award for Outstanding Contributions to Young Adult Literature, Don Gallo is one of the country's leading authorities on books for teenagers and the nation's foremost anthologist of short stories for young people. Among his award-winning anthologies are *Destination Unexpected, First Crossing, On the Fringe, No Easy Answers, Time Capsule,* and *Sixteen,* which is considered one of the 100 Best of the Best Books for Young Adults published in the last third of the twentieth century. A former junior high school teacher and a university professor of English, he currently works as an editor, writer, *English Journal* columnist, workshop presenter, and interviewer of notable authors for the Authors4Teens website. Although this resident of Solon, Ohio, says he has no debilitating fears, he does admit to having been a bit claustrophobic immediately after surviving heart surgery a few years ago. Most of all, he's happy that he does not suffer from arachibutyrophobia, since peanut butter and jelly on crackers is part of his lunch almost every day.

COMMON AND UNCOMMON PHOBIAS

ablutophobia fear of bathing

acarophobia itching

achluophobia darkness (also *lygophobia* and *nyctophobia*)

acrophobia heights (also *altophobia* and *hypsiphobia*)

agliophobia pain (also *algophobia* and *odynophobia*)

agoraphobia open spaces

agyrophobia crossing the street (also *dromophobia*)

ailurophobia cats (also *aelurophobia, elurophobia,* and *felinophobia*)

alektorophobia chickens

amaxophobia riding in a car

androphobia men (also *arrhenphobia*)

anthophobia flowers

apiphobia bees (also *melissophobia*)

arachibutyrophobia peanut butter sticking to the roof of one's mouth

arachnophobia spiders

astraphobia lightning (also *astrapophobia*)

atychiphobia failure (also *kakorrhaphiophobia*)

automatonophobia ventriloquist's dummies

Common and Uncommon Phobias

automysophobia being dirty

aviophobia flying (also *aviatophobia* and *pteromerhanophobia*)

batrachophobia amphibians

belonephobia knives, needles, pins, and other pointed objects (also *aichmophobia* and *enetophobia*)

bibliophobia books

brontophobia thunder and lightning

bufonophobia toads

cacophobia ugliness

caligynephobia beautiful women (also *venustraphobia*)

catoptrophobia mirrors

ceraunophobia thunder (also *tonitrophobia*)

chaetophobia hair

chionophobia snow

chiraptophobia being touched

chronomentrophobia clocks

claustrophobia confining spaces

coimetrophobia cemeteries

coulrophobia clowns

cyberphobia computers (also *computer phobia*)

cyclophobia bicycles

cynophobia dogs

demonophobia demons

dentophobia dentists

didaskaleinophobia school (also *scolionophobia*)

dishabiliophobia undressing in front of others

eisoptrophobia seeing oneself in a mirror

enochlophobia crowds (also *demophobia* and *ochlophobia*)

entomophobia insects (also *insectophobia*)

equinophobia horses (also *hippophobia*)

ereuthrophobia blushing or the color red (also *erythrophobia*)

frigophobia cold

galeophobia sharks (also *selachophobia*)

gamophobia marriage

genuphobia knees

gephyrophobia crossing bridges

glossophobia speaking in public

graphophobia writing

gymnophobia nudity

gynephobia women (also *gynophobia*)

hadephobia hell (also *stygiophobia*)

heliophobia the sun

hemophobia blood

herpetophobia reptiles

homichlophobia fog (also *nebulaphobia*)

homophobia homosexuality

hydrophobia water

iatrophobia doctors

ichthyophobia fish

isolophobia being alone

kenophobia empty spaces

keraunothnetophobia falling man-made satellites

lachanophobia vegetables

ligyrophobia loud noises (also *phonophobia*)

linonophobia string

logophobia words (also *verbophobia*)

lutraphobia otters

mageirocophobia cooking

mechanophobia machines

melophobia music

metrophobia poetry

misophobia dirt or germs (also *rupophobia*)

musophobia mice

mycophobia mushrooms

mycrophobia small things

necrophobia death (also *thanatophobia*)

noctiphobia night

nosocomephobia hospitals

obesophobia gaining weight

odontophobia teeth or dental surgery

ombrophobia rain

ophidiophobia snakes

ophthalmophobia being stared at

ornithophobia birds

ouranophobia heaven (also *uranophobia*)

pagophobia ice or frost

panophobia fear of everything (also *pantophobia* and *polyphobia*) *papyrophobia* paper

pediophobia dolls

pedophobia children

phasmophobia ghosts

philemaphobia kissing

philophobia falling in love

phobophobia fear/phobias

placophobia tombstones

pogonophobia beards

pteronophobia feathers

pupaphobia puppets

pyrophobia fire

ranidaphobia frogs

rhytiphobia getting wrinkles

samhainophobia Halloween

sciophobia shadows

scoleciphobia worms (also *vermiphobia*)

scriptophobia writing in public

selenophobia the moon (also *lunaphobia*)

sesquipedalophobia long words (also *hippopotomonstro-
    sesquippedaliophobia*)

somniphobia sleep

spheksophobia wasps

stenophobia narrow places

tachophobia speed

technophobia technology

teleophobia definite plans

telephonophobia telephone

testophobia taking tests

thermophobia heat

triskaidekaphobia the number 13

trypanophobia injections

vaccinophobia vaccinations

wiccaphobia witches

xanthophobia the color yellow

xenophobia strangers

xylophobia forests

xyrophobia razors

zoophobia animals

SOURCES

Doctor, Ronald M., and Ada P. Kahn.
The Encyclopedia of Phobias, Fears, and Anxieties.
2nd ed. New York: Facts on File, 2000.

Did You Know?
http://www.didyouknow.cd/phobias/phobias.htm

The Phobia List
http://www.phobialist.com

The 24-Hour Phobia Clinic
http://www.changethatsrightnow.com/phobia_list_of_all_
phobias.asp?PhobiaID=1944&DID=6542